Death Wears A Crimson Hat

The Magnolia Bluff Crime Chronicles Book 1

CW Hawes

CWH Books Katy, TX

ISBN: 978-1-942376-39-2

Cover art by Wyldwood Books

To The Underground Authors,
who took my harebrained idea and turned it into a real town.

Become a VIP Reader

If you're looking for humorous, suspense-filled entertainment, with plenty of thrills and spills, I invite you to become one of my VIP Readers.

You'll get the book *Vampire House and Other Early Cases of Justinia Wright, P.I.* and a monthly email letting you know what other goodies are in the works, as well as curated good reads. And you'll be the first to know about the next release in the Magnolia Bluff Crime Chronicles!

Sign up today! Just tap, click, or scan the QR code!

Contents

Chapter One

THE DRIZZLE MADE A soft tattoo against the windowpane. In another lifetime, a morning such as this would've kept Harry Thurgood under the covers. But not this morning. Not this lifetime. Not the one he was living in Magnolia Bluff, Texas.

He got out of bed, showered, shaved, dressed in his custom made Tom Jones suit, and quickly descended the stairs to the Really Good Wood-Fired Coffee Shop, which he owned, operated, and lived above.

Harry paused a moment in the doorway and let his eyes roam the coffee shop. He was pleased with what he saw.

"What a contrast to the dump this place was three years ago," he murmured.

The tables and chairs he'd brought in from T.A. Tandy in Chicago. Henri Vernier of New York had supplied the flooring and lighting. He was especially pleased with the commissioned paintings by California artists Jane Dillon and Lawrence Pruett that hung on the walls.

A smile formed on his lips. This was a coffee shop worthy of any that could be found in New York, Chicago, or San Francisco.

The smell of high-end brewed coffee filled the air, and he heard Miguel, his cook, singing a song in Spanish. Miguel had been a good find, and, being a second generation native of Magnolia Bluff, had helped Harry acclimate at least to some degree to the small town.

"Good morning, Miguel," he called out as he stepped out onto the floor.

"Good morning, Mr. Thurgood. John Paul has already been here with the egg delivery."

Harry stepped to the window behind the counter that looked into the kitchen.

Miguel continued, "I roasted three pounds of the Kenya Double A. While the fire is still hot, do you want to roast anything else?" The voice had a decidedly south of the border accent. Harry supposed that came from speaking Spanish before English.

"The Celebes Kalossi. Three pounds."

"Sure thing, Mr. Thurgood. I left a message for Mr. Bauer asking him to deliver a load of hickory. We're running low."

"Thanks, Miguel. And on that note, a new day begins."

"Si, Mr. Thurgood."

Harry turned around. "Can't disappoint the regulars," he murmured, and added, "All three of them," as he made sure the Windsor knot in his tie felt perfect.

He heard a tapping, and, through the glass, he could see one of his regulars, like clockwork, waiting for him to open.

He unlocked the door, held it open for her, and said, "Good morning, Reverend Cole. I see you're dressed for the weather."

Ember Cole closed her umbrella. "Are you making a joke about my attire?"

"Who me?" Harry pulled the door closed to keep the January chill on the other side. "Nah. I wouldn't do that."

"Yeah, right." Ember walked to the counter and took a seat on one of the stools. "Besides, I thought men liked women in black."

He walked to the end of the counter and came up the other side to stand opposite her. "We do. Just not the black you're wearing. Want your usual?"

"Yes, sir, I do." She set her saturno on the counter. It was one of those hats that Catholic priests sometimes wore.

Harry called back to Miguel, "One fried egg sandwich on wheat toast for the Reverend."

"Si, Mr. Thurgood."

Harry poured coffee into a heavy ceramic cup, added lots of cream and two sugars, and set it before his friend.

"I hope you like Java Plantation. That's what I'm going with this morning."

"Don't know that I've ever had that before, but I'm sure it will be good. You've never yet served a bad cup of coffee."

"Thank you for that. What's on your schedule today, Em? A funeral?"

"Will you cut it out? Black befits my position as a member of the clergy. It has nothing to do with me performing a funeral, or my outlook on life, or my emotional state. It's just my uniform."

Harry held up his hands. "Okay. Sorry. Didn't know you'd gotten out of bed on the wrong side this morning. Or did your cat throw up on you, again?"

"Are you always this cheery before noon? No, wait. I'm here often enough to know you aren't. So what gives today?"

"Okay, ya got me. I'm only cheery when I see you."

"Uh-huh." She took a sip of coffee to hide her smile, then lowered the cup, holding it with both hands. "This is good. Just the usual on today's agenda. Hospital visit. Work on my sermon. Some neighborhood visitation. Nothing out of the ordinary."

"Be here for lunch?"

She set the cup down, and leaned forward, gazing into Harry's eyes. "And what if I said no?"

"I'd cry me a river."

Ember sat up straight, rolled her eyes, and picked up her coffee cup.

"Order up for the Reverend."

Harry retrieved the plate and set it in front of Ember, along with a knife, fork, and spoon all rolled up in a paper napkin.

"There you go, ma'am."

Ember began eating and, after a moment, Harry said, "So why is it you come here every morning instead of going to the Silver Spoon or the Flower? Everyone's there. You'd have the low down on what's going on around town in five minutes flat. Wait. Don't tell me. It's my coffee." He gave her a big grin.

"I didn't order a side of ham."

Harry laughed, and then became serious. "Is it the coffee?"

Ember smiled. "In part. You brew up some pretty exotic stuff." She paused, then continued, "To tell the truth, I feel out of place over there at the Spoon. All men. They clam up when they see me. And it's no better at the B and B. We're outsiders, you and me. Small towns don't trust outsiders."

"No, they don't."

"And they especially don't trust women ministers."

"But this is a college town."

"It is. Doesn't make the people here forward thinking." She looked at her watch. "Oh, shoot. I'm going to be late for my haircut appointment."

Harry reached behind him and grabbed a styrofoam box. “Here.”

“Thanks, Harry.” She picked up the box, put her sandwich in it, plopped her hat on her head, grabbed her umbrella, and turned to go.

“Wait.”

Ember turned back to face him.

“Here.” He reached over and tilted her saturno so it sat at a more rakish angle on her head. “There.”

“Very funny, mister.” The smile, though, belied the sternness of her voice.

“See ya later.”

“Bye, Harry.”

She turned and left. Harry watched her go, and then collected her dishes.

The Reverend Ember Cole is a mighty fine woman, he thought. *Makes me want to have a soul so she could save it.*

Chapter Two

THE REVEREND EMBER COLE walked through the door of the Really Good Wood-Fired Coffee Shop at precisely five minutes after one and froze.

There, in the corner, Mary Lou Fight was holding court with the five members of her Crimson Hat Society, all decked out in their red hats, yellow feather boas, and indigo attire.

Mary Lou and her husband Gunter were prominent, very prominent members of Ember's church. And an unrelenting source of grief for her.

Scarlett Hayden saw her and waved.

The only honest one in the bunch, Ember thought and waved back. She proceeded to the counter where Harry was standing at the end opposite from where Mary Lou was holding court. The eyes of the Queen of the Crimson Hats followed Ember.

The Reverend took a seat, and Harry handed her a menu. "I know you don't need this, but ol' eagle-eye is watching us."

"And I bet her mouth is still talking to her flock."

"It is. And was that a note of disdain I heard? Isn't that a sin or something?"

"That woman makes the Devil look like Gabriel."

"You know what they say: there's telephone, telegraph, but don't tell Mary Lou."

Ember smiled. "I don't think that's how it goes."

"But it's the truth."

"That it is."

"You want your usual?"

"Sure. Especially since this drizzle isn't letting up."

Harry turned towards the window to the kitchen. "Bowl of chili, with cornbread for the Reverend."

"Si, Mr. Thurgood."

He turned back to Ember. "You having a good day so far?"

"Not bad. Just wish I'd hear more good news. People tend to see me when they need something fixed."

"That's usually how it goes. When you're in the fix-it business, that is."

"Ain't that the truth."

"Order up for the Reverend."

Harry grabbed Ember's plate of cornbread and bowl of chili and set them before her, then added a set of tableware and a napkin.

"Thanks, Harry."

"Water? Or would you like to be more adventurous today?"

"Water's fine."

Harry filled a glass and set it before her.

Between spoons of chili, Ember asked, "What are the Hats doing here? It's not their regular day."

"Don't know. Hang on. I'm being flagged. Probably another chamomile tea, with soy milk and Allulose. I'll be back."

Ember didn't watch Harry Thurgood walk over to the table of Hats because she knew Mary Lou would be watching to see if she did.

A spoon of chili made its way to Ember's mouth. *That woman makes my blood boil,* she thought as she swallowed the chili. *Just something else I need to leave in your capable hands, Jesus. But I do wish you'd do something real quick.*

Harry left the table, stopped at the window to give the orders to Miguel, and returned to where Ember was sitting.

"How is it," he said, "that information just flows to some people and usually to the people you don't want to have it?"

"Wish I knew. Did they say something critical about us over there?"

"Mary Lou made a couple of suggestive comments about you and me. I told her that I needed to keep my very few customers satisfied, and if she could send more business my way, I'd give her and her group free drinks next time."

"What did she say?"

"Purred on as to how they all would do their best for me."

"Good luck with that. Since you didn't get a bank loan through her husband's bank, she'd just as soon see you go under as to help you out."

"Maybe. But then where would Charmaine get her chamomile tea?"

"As if Mary Lou gave a damn about that."

"Whoa, Reverend! I'll pretend I didn't hear that."

Ember smiled. "I shouldn't let her get under my skin. It's just that she makes life very difficult for me. And can make it worse, if she chose to do so." She paused, then added, "God, I hate walking on eggshells."

"Let's change the subject. You doing anything later? We could get a bite to eat and watch a movie at my place. Or yours."

"I'd like that, Harry. But..."

"Yeah, yeah. You have to be above reproach so gossip hags like Mary Lou won't have any ammunition."

"Sorry. You see, every year I'm up for review. I don't want to get sent somewhere else. I... Well, you know... I like it here."

"In spite of being an outsider?"

"There are some nice people here. And it's beautiful country."

"Gotcha." He paused, then said, "If you change your mind..."

Ember nodded.

"Order up, Mr. Thurgood."

Harry took the tray to the Crimson Hat table, and Ember put a spoonful of chili in her mouth. She slowly chewed and thought of Harry asking her out. He was definitely an attractive man. Tall. With that wavy blond hair. Probably in his forties.

A man of the world interested in me. She smiled, but a frown quickly pushed the smile away. *Mary Lou. If it wasn't for her, I could go out with him. But that will never happen.*

She took a bite of cornbread. *But if we did go out, nothing could come of it. We can only be friends. Because if he knew...*

Ember didn't want to go down that road, not now, and quickly finished her lunch. She got up, fished a twenty out of her purse, remembering she hadn't paid for breakfast, and put it on the counter next to her plate. She smoothed her skirt, cast a glance at the Hats, and saw Mary Lou looking at her. She smiled at the Queen of the Magnolia Bluff Society of Gossips, Backbiters, and Character Assassins.

Once outside, she stopped, took hold of the cross that hung on a chain around her neck, and whispered. "Anytime, Lord. Anytime."

Chapter Three

LOUISA MIDDLEBROOK TOOK OFF her garish crimson hat and yellow feather boa, put them on the coffee table, and dropped into her favorite chair by the fireplace in the living room.

She felt sick. The bile burned in her throat. She got up, walked down the hall to the bathroom, dumped four antacids into her palm, put the bottle away, and conveyed the tablets to her mouth. She chewed, swallowed, and slowly made her way back to the living room.

Once again seated in her favorite chair, Louisa leaned her head back and closed her eyes.

The Reverend Ember Cole had visited twice, just a pleasant social call. After all, she and Ron were churched, members of the First Baptist Church of Magnolia Bluff. Ember, though, had made it clear she wasn't out to steal from another shepherd's flock. She just wanted to meet the people in town and introduce herself.

Louisa liked Ember right away. She wasn't anything like that godless liberal who'd been the pastor of the Methodist Church before her. Why Louisa even thought Ember might be born again, although Ron found it difficult to believe that any born again woman could be a minister.

And both times she'd visited, Louisa had given Reverend Cole a couple dozen porterhouse and ribeye steaks. "That's prize winnin' meat from Ron's herd. Best in the Hill Country," she'd proudly declared.

Now, according to Mary Lou, Reverend Cole had compromised her office. And Mary Lou would know. She knew everything about everybody. And Mary Lou wasn't alone. Charmaine Adler could've sworn she saw Harry Thurgood's

BMW parked across the street from the Methodist parsonage a couple weeks back. And late at night, at that.

Louisa never doubted Mary Lou. After all, she'd been right about that city councilwoman and the city treasurer a few years back. And then there was the high school teacher who got one of his students pregnant, and Mary Lou knew all about the abortion and her seeing that therapist at the college.

No, Mary Lou *knew*. And her knowledge knew no bounds. So how could she be wrong about Ember Cole? Well, she couldn't. She just couldn't be wrong.

Which meant Reverend Cole was guilty of sin, and Mary Lou's prophecy would come to pass: "We'll be getting a new minister at the church come July."

But what made Louisa sick to her stomach was the order to keep an eye on Harry Thurgood and the Reverend.

"I need plenty of evidence to persuade the Personnel Team and Texas Conference Cabinet that she's a sinner. And I *know* I can count on my fellow Crimson Hatters to help me," Mary Lou had said.

Louisa got up from her chair and walked out to the kitchen, took out the carton of milk from the fridge and poured herself a glass. She got a package of fudge sandwich cookies from the cupboard, opened the bag, and began eating cookies one after the other, in between sips of milk.

She stared out the kitchen window. Mary Lou had been good to her. Had invited her, her of all people, Louisa *Nobody* Middlebrook to become a member of the prestigious Crimson Hat Society. And if Louisa wanted to remain a member, then she had to do Mary Lou's bidding. And she had. She'd given up her old friends and made new ones. Ones that were socially acceptable. People who met with Mary Lou's approval. And, because of that, she was no longer a *nobody*. She was a somebody. She was important.

Ever since Mary Lou had chosen her, no one made fun of her weight. No one bullied her, or called her "fatty". Mary Lou had been her mentor. Taught her how to dress, wear her hair. Thanks to Ron, she had money; and Mary Lou had taught her how to make that money work for her to get prestige and influence.

She'd do what Mary Lou asked. She would always do what Mary Lou asked. Because she was never going to be a nobody again.

Chapter Four

SCARLETT HAYDEN MIXED HERSELF a martini and thought about what that bossy cow, Mary Lou Fight, had said at the "emergency" meeting of the Magnolia Bluff Crimson Hat Society.

Because she was hungry, she dropped three olives into her drink and took it to the family room. She set it on the coffee table and stretched out on the couch.

So what if Thurgood and Ember were getting it on? Who really cared? She reached over, picked up her drink, and took a large swallow.

Just because Ember was a minister didn't mean she couldn't enjoy a little nookie every now and then. Hell, who cared if she got laid every night?

Scarlett took another swallow of her drink, and a smile lifted her ruby lips. "Now that Thurgood...," she mused out loud. "He's one guy whose pants I wouldn't mind getting into. Not at all. And that hair..." She shivered with desire.

The smile lingered while she fished an olive out of her drink and ate it; licking the gin and vermouth off her fingers. The young studs from the football team were insatiable and she liked that. They never missed a chance to put one through the uprights. But at forty-eight, she needed to think about the future. Eddie had a good insurance policy and she'd made out quite well when he kicked off. A half-mil in cash and the resort.

"But I bet ol' Harry Thurgood has money *and* knows how to give a girl a good time. I bet he knows how to make love, not just rut like a dog." A dreamy look settled on her face at the thought of Harry Thurgood in her bed. She ate another olive, once again licking the alcohol off her fingers.

"Of course, if he is seeing Ember, which I doubt, Mary Lou has that one all wrong, but if he is, then it wouldn't hurt to get the Reverend out of the way."

She took a large swallow of her drink. "On the other hand, if he isn't boffing the Rev, maybe he's feeling lonesome. Maybe he'd be open to a little entertainment. The kind only a mature woman can provide."

Scarlett smiled. "And once he had a taste of me, he'd forget Ember Cole even existed. That is, if he's even interested in her. And I doubt that he is. She doesn't even look like a woman. Totally shapeless."

She took a sip of her drink. "I'm beginning to really like this idea." She raised her drink. "To the future. And thanks, Mary Lou. Your barking up the wrong tree just might provide me with a very big harvest." She couldn't resist giggling. "Sure, Mary Lou, whatever you say."

She downed the rest of her drink and got up to make another. "Whoever said diamonds are a girl's best friend got it all wrong. It's money. Plain and simple. Cold, hard cash. That's what we love best."

Drink made, she returned to the couch. "That, of course, might not apply when considering that good-looking Harry Thurgood. After all, I've plenty of money, being a rich widow ain't bad; and on Harry Thurgood's arm, being a rich widow would be even better."

***

Across Burnet Reservoir, Jessamine Walter was sipping a Pimm's Winter Cup.

This time Mary Lou has bitten off more than she can chew, she thought. *And when her plan backfires, then I'll be able to maneuver her out of being queen. Besides...* She sipped her drink. *The bitch needs to be taught a lesson. All of these upstarts do.*

A shudder ran through her. *Of all the godforsaken places on this planet, why did Allan have to take a teaching position here? I should be back in Charleston, among my own kind. Mother was right: I should have married Braxton. He at least had good lineage.* Jessamine sighed, finished her drink, and stood.

"This time," she said out loud, "I'm going to have all the fun at Mary Lou's expense. Not that I care two hoots about Mary Lou getting a new Methodist minister. But, as they say, politics makes for strange bedfellows. And, I've had my eye on Ember for a while now. She's such a cutie. Strange bedfellows, indeed."

She smiled, walked to the bar, and poured herself another drink from the pitcher on the warming plate.

The doorbell rang. She looked at her watch, and a smile teased her lips.

That must be Terrell, she thought.

She set her drink down, walked to the front of the house, and answered the door. Before her stood a well-built young man. Powerful. Strong. His dark chocolate skin shone in the light.

"Hi, Mrs. Walter. I'm here to wash and vacuum your car."

Jessamine smiled. "Right on time. Come in. Let me get the keys."

She stepped away from the door, retrieved her key ring, and returned.

"Here you go."

"Thanks. Do you want me to wax it today?"

"No. Wash and vacuum is fine."

The young man nodded, and left.

Jessamine watched him from a window. He was a fine looking young man. She knew nothing about football, but liked watching him power his way through the opposing team when he had the ball. Powerful. She liked that.

After a few moments, she returned to the bar. Drink in hand, she returned to the sofa, her mind back on business.

"I think the first thing I'll do when I'm queen is get rid of that damn yellow boa Mary Lou insists we all wear. What a ghastly color."

Jessamine raised the glass to her lips and took a sip. "The second thing I'll do is invite Ember Cole to join the Crimson Hat Society. The more, the merrier, as we dance on Mary Lou's grave. And once she realizes who to thank for keeping her job..."

She smiled, raised her glass in a toast, and said, "Here's to us, and those like us. Few though they be."

Chapter Five

THE MEMBERS OF THE Crimson Hat Society had departed at 2:30, and a half-hour later Harry Thurgood locked the door and flipped the sign from open to closed.

While he was counting the day's receipts, Miguel cooked Harry's supper, cleaned up the kitchen, and then left for the day.

When he'd finished counting the money, three times for good measure, Harry looked at the meager pile of checks, charge slips, cash, and coins.

"Looks like I'm going to have to give you another cash infusion before the month is out," he said to the empty coffee shop. "Miguel's a good worker, but he does appreciate getting paid. So do the wholesalers and suppliers, for that matter. Especially Elder Smythe."

Harry sighed, and put the day's receipts in a bag. He looked out the window. The drizzle had stopped so he wouldn't need his umbrella. He grabbed his porkpie, put it on his head, and walked across the town square to the bank. On the north end of the square, as imposing as a medieval cathedral, was the courthouse.

He cast a glance its way and snorted. Justice and miscarriages of justice. Like all of the backroom dealings in response to that big box store's request for permission to build. Which they didn't get, thank God. Or all of the legal maneuvering over that doggone strip mall. None of it really had anything to do with justice or what's right, it all had to do with greed and money.

On the south end stood the library. Not as imposing as the courthouse, but probably much more important. The repository of the town's history. A bastion of knowledge and information. The library was a good thing.

And then there was the bank. Gunter Fight's bank. Mary Lou probably pumped her husband for information, aka gossip. That was without a doubt how she knew all about the Really Good's cash flow, or more accurately, the lack thereof.

He entered the building and walked up to a teller window.

"A good afternoon to you, Sarah Jean." He tipped his hat to her, and a smile appeared on her face.

"Hello, Mr. Thurgood."

He said hello back, as he handed her the bag.

"Your day's receipts?"

He nodded.

She opened the bag, counted the checks and cash, and compared her tally with his deposit slip. "Looks good. Anything else?"

"No. Have a good evening."

"Thanks. You, too."

He raised his hat to her, turned, and left.

Back out on the street, Harry looked across the green at the coffee shop and decided he didn't want to go home quite yet. He looked at his watch. Four-thirty. A little early to hit O'Gara's.

"I wonder just how far Mary Lou's tentacles reach?" he murmured to himself. He crossed the street to the green, took his phone out of his suit coat pocket, and told it to call "Em."

After four rings, he heard, "Hello, Harry. I think it best if I say no."

"Say no to what? I haven't said anything yet."

"Good. I don't want you to say anything I might say yes to."

"What's the matter? Did I say or do something you don't like?"

"No, you didn't. It's not you. It's us."

"We're an us?"

"Well, no, we aren't and I want it to stay that way."

"I have no idea what's going on, Em, but maybe we should talk."

"We are talking."

"In person."

"I don't think that's a good idea, Harry. If people see us, they'll talk, And right now I don't need that."

"Okay. I get it. This has something to do with the Queen of Dirt and her minions, doesn't it?"

"That's a good one. Did you make that up?"

"I did. Just now. Look, how about you drive out to some place and I'll meet you there and then we'll go to Austin. We can have supper and you can tell me all about it."

"Not a good idea, Harry."

"Didn't I learn in Sunday school that Bible verse, 'Greater is he that is within you, than he that's within Mary Lou?'"

Ember burst out laughing.

"Glad I can make you laugh, Em."

Her laughter subsided. "Thank you. I needed that."

"So why don't I meet you in the college parking lot. Will that work? Or do you have a better place?"

"I don't know why I'm letting you talk me into this." There was a pause, and then she said, "Yes, I have a better idea. Pick me up at the cemetery."

"Huh. That's novel. You don't think Mary Lou communes with the dead?"

"Being a bloodsucking vampire, she probably does. But she definitely prefers the living."

"Wow. I think you're going to have to go to confession."

"I'm Methodist. I talk directly with God."

"Hope he's talking back."

"Ha, ha. Meet me at the cemetery at eight. And I still don't know why I'm letting you talk me into this. It really isn't a good idea."

"If it isn't a good idea, then why are you giving in?"

"Because, right now, you're the only person I trust, and I'd really like to talk to someone who comprehends the definition of the word discretion."

Chapter Six

HARRY DIDN'T RECOGNIZE THE woman when he parked in the cemetery parking lot. His headlights illuminated a tall woman standing under the oak. She was wearing a long white raincoat, tan newsboy cap, with blond locks poking out from under it, platform stiletto heels, and she carried a large bag that hung from her shoulder. She looked like someone from... Well, he wasn't sure. But she sure as hell didn't look like the Reverend Ember Cole.

However, her text message proved him wrong, and he unlocked the passenger door for her.

She got in, told him to get going, and he did, staying on the residential streets.

"You always just so happen to have on hand a blond wig and platform shoes?"

"It's a long story, and one I'm not going to tell you. At least anytime soon."

"Okay. Suit yourself. So what's going on?"

He turned onto State Highway 113, headed for Austin, and when Magnolia Bluff was only visible in the rearview mirror, Ember began.

"I got a call at the church from Effie Snyder. She said Opal Nussbaum told her she'd overheard Betty Sue Fernhope, she's one of the Hats."

Harry nodded.

"She overheard Betty Sue make the implication that there'd be a new minister at the church this year. Meaning my church. Apparently, Betty Sue didn't realize Opal was just two chairs down from her at the beauty salon."

"Let's see, that's..." Harry paused, counting on the fingers of his right hand, before continuing, "That's third-hand information. How reliable can that be?"

"Well, it was Effie who told me, and she doesn't make things up."

"How reliable is Opal?"

"I don't know. I don't know her all that well. But why would she lie about what Betty Sue said?"

"Maybe she didn't. Maybe she just didn't hear it very clearly and filled in the blanks."

"I suppose..."

"But, then again, maybe the ol' Dirt Queen is gunning for you."

"Oh, she hasn't liked me since I arrived. Mary Lou has made it very clear that while she believes men and women are equal, there are just some things better done by a man — and being a minister is one of them."

"I see. So she has us engaging in a little connubial dancing in order to compromise your integrity."

"That's how I see it."

"And even though it's not true, once doubt enters people's minds..."

"Exactly. I'm finished. What parent will want the harlot near their children? Who will listen to the strumpet in the pulpit?"

"I thought Methodists were pretty liberal."

"Well, Harry, there's liberal and then there's liberal. If you get my drift."

"Gotcha. What's good for the goose isn't necessarily permitted to the gander."

"Except I'm the goose, but yeah."

Harry chuckled.

"What's so funny?"

"It's that old song. 'And he's suspected of making whoopee.' Only in this case, the suspect's a she."

"I don't get it."

"An old song from the thirties, I believe. Making whoopee is sex. The song is about all the trouble sex causes. Look it up. It's hilarious."

"That's okay. I'll take your word for it. So what are we going to do about Mary Lou?"

"Seems to me she's just like the Bismarck and we gotta cut her down."

"Is that another corny song reference?"

"I don't know about corny, but it's from a song."

"Some help you are."

"Hey." He reached over and squeezed her hand. "We'll come up with something."

"I hope so. Because I'm scared Mary Lou is going to take my church away from me."

"Look, Rev, maybe this is the time you need to start revving up the prayer machine. Get a little divine aid. You know, a plague for one or something."

Ember laughed. "Honestly, Harry. A plague for one. Although flies might be fitting. Or hailstones."

"That's the spirit!"

"Seriously, though, you're right: I need to trust God on this. He knows what's best, and I should be seeking His guidance."

"But we can't leave everything to him. Doesn't it say somewhere in the Good Book that God helps those who help themselves?"

Ember laughed. "No, it doesn't. But He doesn't expect us to do nothing, either. We just have to do the best we can and trust in Him that it will all turn out for the best."

Harry let that comment sit for a moment, then said to himself, *That may be okay for you, Ember, but it's not okay for me. Very few things turn out for the best unless we guide them in that direction.*

Chapter Seven

For a Wednesday night, Albert's Steakhouse was busy. Harry and Ember sat in the bar. He nursed a gin rickey, and she a French 75 mocktail, and made small talk for twenty minutes until they were shown to their table in an out of the way corner of the restaurant.

While looking at their menus, Ember said, "We're kind of off by ourselves here. Do you think this is a good idea?"

"With that wig and hat you're, plus those platform shoes, and that ridiculously oversized handbag, I don't think your mother would recognize you."

"Harry, thank you. You've been a good friend, and, well, I, uh, well, I don't want to ruin that."

"Sounds good to me. Are you by any chance trying to tell me you're going to start making coffee at home?"

She laughed an exasperated little laugh. "You're not making this easy for me."

"Okay, how about this? I like you. And you like me. I like you a lot, and I think you like me a lot. We're friends who enjoy each other's company. We're friends with benefits and the benefit is that we are there to support each other. Which is quite a big benefit. How's that?"

Ember smiled. "Thanks, Harry. Thanks for understanding."

"Don't mention it."

The waiter arrived, took their orders, and departed.

"What do we do about Mary Lou?" Ember asked.

"I'm not sure. Bullies, though, usually back down when they meet determined opposition."

"As I understand it, no one's ever succeeded in standing up to her. She knows too much dirt."

"Not about me, she doesn't."

The waiter arrived with the wine, an old vine red zinfandel. Harry smelled the cork, tasted the sample, and gave his approval. The waiter poured wine into their glasses and left the bottle on the table.

"And how is it you're lucky enough to fly under her radar?" Ember took a sip of wine. "Wow, this is really good stuff. Sure beats what comes in those boxes."

"Boxes?" Harry shook his head, then smiled. "Don't like it too much or we'll have to add wino to your growing list of sins."

"That's all I'd need. So how do you do it? And you don't, actually. Now that I think about it."

"No, I don't. But it's nothing she can actually use against me. All the Queen of Dirt has on me is that the coffee shop doesn't make money. Which means I must have a source of funding to keep the place afloat. A source other than Fight's bank. Which is true, I do. No one knows anything about me prior to my arrival in Magnolia Bluff. And I know that bugs Mary Lou to no end."

Ember nodded. "Like you, my past, at least some of it, is a closed book. But being a minister makes me vulnerable to even the slightest insinuations. I'm held to a different standard."

"But unlike me, you got the Big Guy upstairs on your side."

The waiter arrived with their salads and departed.

"Tell you what, Ember."

"What?"

"You pray to the Big Guy, and I'll deal with Mary Lou. I probably speak her language better than you do. What do you say?"

"Harry, I'm not—"

He held up his hand. "The words are 'thank you.'"

She smiled. "Okay. Thank you, Mr. Thurgood."

"You're welcome, Ms. Cole. Now that we have that settled, can we talk about something else?"

"Sure. I'd love to."

***

After dinner, they took the long way back to Magnolia Bluff and finally arrived at the cemetery at five to midnight.

Harry couldn't remember the last time he'd had such an enjoyable dinner date although technically, he supposed, it wasn't a date. Just two friends getting together for a meal. Not that he wouldn't love to date the Reverend Ember Cole. But that wasn't going to happen. At least not in the near future.

Back at his apartment above the coffee shop, he filled and lit his pipe. He made himself a Corpse Reviver No.1 and sat in his favorite rocker-recliner and gently rocked back and forth. He found the action soothing, comforting.

Leaning his head back, he closed his eyes. "Well, Watson," he said out loud, "we have ourselves a three-pipe problem for sure. How do I do unto Mary Lou Fight, the Queen of Dirt, before she does unto the Reverend?"

He sipped his drink, and smoked his pipe, and went over in his mind everything he could possibly think of that had anything even remotely to do with Mary Lou. When his glass was empty and his pipe smoked out, he made himself a fresh drink and filled another pipe.

Somewhere around one in the morning, he repeated both actions a third time. And by a quarter to two, with pipe and glass empty, Harry Thurgood had the beginnings of a plan.

He smiled to himself and called it a night.

Getting into bed, he thought of Ember and said to the darkness, "I hope she dreams a little dream of me."

Chapter Eight

THURSDAY MORNING. DAWN'S EARLY light tinged the horizon, but it was still dark behind the Really Good. Harry flipped on the light and opened the door.

"Good morning, Elder Smythe. Where's John Paul?"

"Not feeling well this morning. Out with his cousin last night and came back not feeling well."

"That's too bad. Hope it's nothing serious."

"Either the flu or a little food poisoning. Something spoiled will do that to you."

"That it will."

"I have your eggs for you, the vegetables, and the goat cheese. Might I interest you in a few chickens? Young roosters, and a couple old hens for stewing. They'd make good soup, too."

Harry thought a moment. "I could put chicken salad and chicken noodle soup on the menu. Sure. Two roosters and the two hens."

"Thank you kindly, Mr. Thurgood."

Harry took out his wallet, and Smythe gave him the invoice slip. After giving the minister a sufficient number of bills to cover the cost of the delivery, plus a small tip, Harry returned to the front of the coffee shop and began putting flatware and napkins on the tables.

***

After her devotions and prayers, Ember walked to the Really Good for her breakfast. She enjoyed the exercise most mornings, as it gave her time to reflect on the upcoming day.

It was also when Magnolia Bluff was at its quietest, and she relished the quiet.

The sky was light, but the sun wasn't up yet. Nevertheless, the birds were starting in early. There was the long call of the cardinal, ending with that distinctive *chu, chu, chu* sound. The cedar waxwings and their short, thin, high-pitched call. There was the smell of someone's wood fire.

She loved observing the lines of the naked trees. Seeing their bare form that was less clear when they were in leaf. There was something elementally majestic in the form of bare trees. In a way, not very different than the human body. Although, now that she was a Christian, she knew she was supposed to see the naked body as sinful. And perhaps it was outside of a husband and wife seeing each other, but nakedness could be a beautiful thing. Although in her past it was usually perverted.

"Dwell on what is lovely," she reminded herself, and switched her attention to the clouds catching the light of the morning sun.

She reached the sidewalk of the downtown area and noted that the pigeons were up early; but there wasn't a single person about, and that she thought was somewhat unusual.

When she reached the Really Good, she paused a moment to savor the coffee aroma coming from the place, then opened the door and entered.

She greeted Harry and commented on the emptiness of his shop. "I mean, look, even Fergus isn't here, and he's here most mornings."

That Harry would give a free breakfast to the town drunk whenever he showed up was proof to Ember of Harry's innate goodness. *We need more people like Harry Thurgood*, she thought.

"Quiet morning," he replied.

"I didn't see anybody out on the sidewalk either."

"As I said, quiet morning. We get those sometimes."

"I suppose."

"Your usual? Or are you up for something adventurous?"

Ember smiled. "I'll take my usual."

"Alright, one usual coming up."

Harry passed the order on to Miguel, while he got Ember's coffee.

When he set the cup in front of her, she said, "You have any idea as to what you're going to say to Mary Lou?"

"Not that I'm going to tell you. The less you know about my plans, the better."

Ember chuckled and took a sip of coffee. "That sounds sinister."

"In some circles in would be. In others, just business as usual."

"What did you do before you came here?"

It was Harry's turn to chuckle. "Remember last night? You said you weren't going to tell me about your weird outfit, at least anytime soon?"

She nodded.

"Consider that my answer too."

"I see. I didn't mean to pry."

"I know. For now, we'll keep our pasts in the past. Deal?"

She smiled. "Deal."

Miguel announced that Ember's breakfast was ready, and Harry served it to her.

In between bites of her egg sandwich, she mused aloud that perhaps Mary Lou had organized some kind of boycott against him. "You know, try to drive you out of town. Or to the bank."

Harry chuckled at her suggestion. "All I can say is that if she has that kind of power, then maybe she should go into politics."

Ember wrinkled her nose. "If she did, I think I'd request a position out of state."

"At least she'd be out of your hair. She'd be too busy creating havoc in Austin."

"That's a nightmare I don't want to even think about."

Their conversation shifted to things about town, and when Ember had finished her breakfast, she thanked Harry once again for the previous night's dinner and told him she'd see him later.

From the coffee shop, she walked over to the building housing the *Magnolia Bluff Chronicle*. She said hello to Neal, the publisher, on his way out the door and gave Rebecca, the ad manager, her sermon title to update the church's ad.

"Have you heard the big news?" Rebecca asked.

"No. What's going on?"

"Hattie Bauer and Jake Schwartz found Louisa Middlebrook's body in the cemetery."

"Her body? You mean she's dead?"

"Uh-huh. That's where Neal's headed. Kind of ironic leaving a dead body in the cemetery."

"I guess it is at that. How did she die?"

"Don't know. The word is she was murdered."

"Murdered? Here in town?"

"Apparently. Neal said other than the annual May killing we haven't had a murder in years. This'll be big news. Sell a lot of papers."

"Oh my. This is awful. I just saw her yesterday. At the Really Good. The Hats were having a meeting."

"Looks like Mary Lou is going to have to find a replacement."

"I guess so. Wow. Thanks for the update."

"Sure. No problem." A smile lifted the corners of Rebecca's lips. "You going to check it out?"

"Yeah, I am. I should call her pastor just to make sure he knows."

"Oh, he probably does. Might even be down there by now."

"That's true. He might already be there. Thanks again, Rebecca. See ya."

Ember left the *Chronicle* office and briskly walked to the parsonage where she got her electric moped and rode down to the cemetery.

When she arrived, she saw Logan Ytzen and Nick Vandegan keeping the gawkers on the other side of the yellow crime scene tape.

"Looks like half the town is here," Ember muttered.

She parked the moped and walked up to Logan.

"Mornin', Reverend."

"Good morning, Logan. May I ask what's going on?"

"As if you didn't already know." A smile touched Logan's lips.

"Was is it really Louisa Middlebrook they found?"

"Detective Sovern told us to keep a lid on it. He and Deputy Detective Phil West are checking things out."

Ember waved towards the crowd. "I think it's a little late to put a lid on it, don't you?"

Logan laughed. "Small towns. Don't ya just love 'em?"

"Best communication networks on the planet. Is there any way I can see the body? Is Chris Hayes here? He was her pastor."

"Reverend Hayes isn't here. At least, I haven't seen him." Logan turned to the other officer. "Hey, Nick, you seen Rev. Hayes around?"

"Nope," Nick replied.

Ember said, "I might be able to provide comfort to her family. Be helpful if I knew something."

Logan nodded, said, "Hang on a minute," and walked off into the cemetery.

Behind her, Ember could hear the chatter. A few were even taking pictures with their phones.

"Bunch of ghouls," she muttered.

Rachel Sternbach sidled up to her, and said, "Isn't this just awful? Poor Louisa. Cut down in her prime. Why would anyone want to hurt her?"

"I have no idea, Mrs. Sternbach."

"I've heard tell that this has something to do with her being one of Mary Lou Fight's hat women."

"Really? Why? What does her being a Hat have to do with anything?"

Before Rachel could reply, Logan returned with a man in his upper forties or lower fifties, wearing a somewhat worn two-piece suit. Glasses sat on the end of his nose, and he held an unlit cigar firmly in his teeth.

Logan said, "Reverend Cole, this is police investigator Reece Sovern. Detective, Reverend Ember Cole of St. Luke's Methodist."

"Pleased to meet you, Reverend. I've seen you about and have heard of you. Always good to know the folks who have the Lord's ear, so to speak. What can I do for you?"

Ember was so mesmerized by the investigator's ability to speak clearly while the cigar stayed completely stationary in the corner of his mouth that she failed to notice the conversational ball was in her court.

"Reverend?" Sovern said.

"Oh, sorry." Ember's face went crimson. "Uh, I was wondering if you could tell me who the victim was. You know, I might have to do grief counseling and I'd like to be prepared."

Sovern pursed his lips and looked at the pine tree that was a dozen feet away. In a moment, his eyes focused back on Ember. He motioned with his head for her to follow, and then his back was moving away from her.

"Your lucky day," Logan said, and lifted the crime scene tape.

Ember passed beneath it, and hurried after the police investigator.

Chapter Nine

HARRY THURGOOD WAS WIPING down tables in preparation for the lunch crowd he hoped would someday appear when Ember Cole burst through the door.

"Whoa, Rev. Take it easy on the hardware."

"Sorry, Harry. Have you heard?"

"Probably not. I'm usually the last to know."

"Louisa Middlebrook is dead."

"Seriously?"

Ember nodded.

"How did it happen?"

"She was run over by a car, or maybe a pickup. But Reece and the JP suspect she was hit on the head first. Then her body was dumped in the cemetery."

"Well, she was going to end up there eventually."

"Harry, that's not nice."

"Sorry. It's true, but I probably shouldn't have said it."

"No, you shouldn't have."

"Her death is going to be fuel for the gossips for weeks, and now Mary Lou will need to find a replacement."

Ember sat at a table. "I met her twice. A very nice person. Gave me loads of steaks both times. I notified Chris Hayes because she went to his church."

"Better he do the funeral than you. Although you're dressed for it."

"Harry, this is not a good time."

"Sorry. Just trying to keep it light. Who would want to kill Louisa of all people?"

"Don't know. Reece Sovern doesn't want to call it murder yet. Not until the autopsy is completed. Her death is officially suspicious."

"That still leaves us with who might want to see her dead. Or could it have been an accident?"

"Sovern doesn't think her death was accidental, and Wylie, the justice of the peace, agrees. Wylie said it would have to be an accident aided by the victim for the tire marks to be where they were. In addition to the head injury. Sovern's just waiting on the autopsy to officially call it murder."

"Unless the autopsy tells him something else."

"Right."

"Does her husband know?"

"Sovern sent a cop to find him so a positive ID can be made, which seems pretty weird since everyone there knew who she was. And at least half the town was there."

"It's government, you know. Cross Ts and dot Is."

"Still, seems a waste of time."

"Government mostly is." He noticed the look on her face. "What? You don't believe me?"

She waved away the question. "Harry, don't laugh, but I prayed God would do something about Mary Lou."

"Seems to me, he missed. Or decided you were praying for the wrong target."

Ember stood, hands on hips. "Harry Thurgood! How can you say something like that?"

He shrugged. "Doesn't it say somewhere in the Good Book that we don't know how to pray, so the Holy Spirit prays on our behalf? You know, so we get it right?"

Ember paused, then said, "Yes, it does. Romans eight. But—"

"Em, I don't think this has anything to do with your prayer. In fact, I'd say God probably shook his head and chalked up your request to you having a bad day. What this does have to do with is someone did not like Louisa Middlebrook. Didn't like her enough, in fact, to end her life."

"But who on earth would want to hurt Louisa? She was harmless."

"To you and me. But not to someone else. And it's Sovern's job to find out who that person is. I'm more interested in who Mary Lou is going to ask to join the Hats and if she's still going to try and oust you from the church. Louisa's death is tragic, but it seems to me you have more important matters demanding your attention."

"I suppose you're right."

"As long as you're here, you want lunch?"
"Sure."
"What would you like?"
"How about a grilled cheese sandwich?"
"One grilled cheese coming right up."

***

When Ember and the four other lunch customers had left, Harry sat at a table in the corner. He ate a slice of cherry pie, acknowledging that Noonan over at Bluff Bakery made the best cherry pie he'd ever eaten, and drank a cup of Columbian light roast coffee.

While eating and drinking, he thought of his plan to get Mary Lou off Ember's back. Would Louisa's death change anything?

Probably not, he thought.

"Nevertheless, I should probably make sure," he said to the now empty plate.

But who to ask? He closed his eyes and ran over a list of possibilities. When he opened them, he sighed.

He picked up his coffee cup, saw that it was empty, and set it back down.

There was only one person he needed to talk to, and that was the Queen of Dirt herself.

Chapter Ten

HARRY THURGOOD DROVE HIS BMW over to Water Street and then up Sandalwood Drive. Sandalwood Drive, that arm of Magnolia Bluff that caressed the northeast shore of Burnet Reservoir and provided an enclave where the town's monied families could live and play and not be sullied by the hoi polloi.

Harry parked his car in front of a large pseudo-plantation-style home. He got out, walked up the flagstone walk, and rang the doorbell. From somewhere deep within the godawful ugly edifice he heard the chime sound.

He was about to press the button a second time when the door opened. A decidedly middle-aged woman, wearing a maid's uniform straight out of a 1940s movie, looked at him and asked what he wanted. Her accent placed the land of her birth south of the border.

"I'd like to see Mrs. Fight. Tell her Harry Thurgood is here to see her."

"Please wait," the maid said and closed the door.

Harry waited for a good six minutes before the door opened and the maid asked him to step inside. He did, she closed the door, and asked him to follow her.

From the large entryway, he followed her through a door on the right into a room that was probably twice the size of his coffee shop. The maid left and closed the door.

A fireplace was along one wall, a white grand piano was at the far end, and an assortment of sofas and chairs formed areas for people to sit and engage in conversation. Paintings hung on the walls, and large windows essentially replaced the walls at the far end of the room.

From one of the sofas in the middle of the room, Mary Lou Fight stood. She wore a cream-colored dress. The only accent

Harry could see was the strand of pearls she wore around her neck.

"Mr. Thurgood, to what do I owe the honor of your visit?"

"I wanted to see how the other half lives."

She arched an eyebrow. "Have a seat." She indicated a chair. Harry walked to it and sat after Mary Lou had returned to her seat on the couch.

"And what do you think, Mr. Thurgood?" she purred.

"What I've always suspected. The other half lives quite well."

"Jesus said that we'll always have the poor with us. I suppose, by implication, that also means the rich will always be with us as well. Wouldn't you rather be rich?"

"I'd rather be happy."

She smiled at his reply and asked if he'd like something to drink. "I'm having tea."

"No, thank you. But you go ahead."

She rang a bell. The maid appeared. "Tea, please, Gabriela." The maid nodded and departed.

She turned back to Harry. "I suppose you heard about Louisa Middlebrook."

"I did. Tragic. Can't figure out why someone would feel the need to kill her."

"She was one of my girls. It is very sad, and I don't understand it either."

"Maybe there is one reason that makes sense."

The maid entered and placed the tray with teapot, cups, and sundry other items on the table by Mary Lou and left.

"You sure you won't have tea?"

Harry held up his hand. "I'm fine, thank you."

"You were saying there is a reason that makes sense?"

"Yes. Perhaps it was a message to you regarding the inadvisability of your current campaign."

"And what campaign would that be?"

"The one to deprive a shepherd of the flock she dearly loves."

"I'm sure I don't know what you're talking about, Mr. Thurgood."

"Oh, I'm sure you do."

"Am I to understand you to be saying that someone, with an animus against me, killed poor Louisa to send me a message? If so, I'm afraid I have no idea what that message would be."

"In a battle, a general may attack an insignificant position. In doing so, he draws his opponent's attention away from the real objective."

Mary Lou poured herself a cup of tea and took a sip. She decided it needed milk and sugar, added both, and took another sip.

"Thank you for the lesson in military strategy. Is there anything else, Mr. Thurgood?"

"I'll be straightforward, Mrs. Fight. Are you familiar with Handel's *Messiah*?"

"Somewhat."

"The text comes from the Bible. There's an Air that fits this situation. I don't know where the text is in the Bible. I suppose it doesn't matter. The Bass sings, 'The kings of the earth rise up, and the rulers take counsel together against the Lord, and against his Anointed.' Then the Tenor sings, 'Thou shalt break them with a rod of iron. Thou shalt dash them to pieces like a potter's vessel.' Now keep in mind, Mrs. Fight, that queen can easily be substituted for king. And that God's rod of iron can break both of them."

Harry stood. "I'll see myself out."

***

Mary Lou watched Harry leave. She raised her teacup to her lips and sipped tea.

Perhaps I underestimated that lounge lizard, she thought.

She took another sip of tea, set the cup in the saucer, and set them on the coffee table.

"Quoting from *Messiah*. Yes, there's more to that Yankee pretty boy than meets the eye."

She stood, walked to one of the floor to ceiling windows, and looked out on her world.

"I think it's time to teach Mr. Thurgood, if that's even his name, a lesson." A smile touched her lips. "Yes, this is a job for Hunter. He'll find all the dirt hiding in your closet Harry Thurgood, and with it — I will break *you*!"

Her laughter filled the room.

Chapter Eleven

The Reverend Ember Cole sat behind her desk in the church office. The receptionist had gone home for the day. Ember was supposed to be working on her sermon, but her mind kept drifting back to Louisa Middlebrook's crushed body.

Finally, she shook her head and pushed her chair away from the desk. "I'm not going to get any work done here. I might as well go home."

She stood, grabbed her hat, and left the church by the back door, making sure to lock it. The parsonage was next door, a mere couple dozen steps away. She unlocked the back door, and stepped in.

"Wilbur, I'm home!" Ember called out.

From somewhere, the gray tabby appeared, rubbing himself against a kitchen cupboard.

Ember hung her hat on a peg by the door, then reached down and picked up her fur baby.

"Were you a good boy while I was gone?"

Wilbur purred, let Ember scratch his neck for all of twenty seconds, and then wiggled his interest to be back on the floor.

She set him down, and, at the same time, the doorbell rang. The cat took off to hide under the couch.

Walking to the front of the house, Ember muttered, "Who could that be?" When she got to the door, she opened it, and found herself face to face with Reece Sovern. He'd opened the screen door.

"Evening, Reverend."

"What can I do for you, Mr. Sovern?"

He held up a sheet of paper. "This here's a warrant for us to search your house, garage, and to take your car for a detailed examination."

"What on earth for?"

"It's come to my attention, that there's some animosity between you and the members of the Crimson Hat Society. Which to my mind gives you a motive in the death of Louisa Middlebrook, and Judge Jones concurs and issued the warrant."

Sovern handed her the paper and motioned for his men to go to work.

"We'll try not to make a mess," the investigator said. "We're looking for specific items. Now if you'll just stand aside, we'll get to work and be out of your hair ASAP."

"What about my car? When will I get that back?"

"If it's clean? Probably Monday."

Ember shook her head. She couldn't believe this was happening. She stuffed the warrant into a suit coat pocket and pulled her phone out of another and told it to call Harry.

***

Ember sat in Harry's BMW, and the two of them watched the tow truck haul away her car.

"I don't know how I'm going to survive this, Harry."

"Look, Em, you didn't do it. Sovern is a good bureaucrat. He's just doing his job. My guess is that Mary Lou, either directly or through the grapevine, put a bug in his ear. And quite honestly, he'd be a fool not to follow up on it."

"I know. But I think I'm finished here. As a pastor that is."

"Oh, ye, of little faith. Shouldn't you be running the rosary or something?"

"I'm not Catholic. But I did say a nice, short and sweet, Protestant prayer."

"There you go. Have faith, my friend."

"Are you a believer, Harry? I don't think you've ever said."

"Depends on what day you ask me."

"That sounds just like you. But thanks for reminding me where my strength lies."

"You need a thicker skin, my friend. Too many Mary Lous are out there who want you for breakfast."

"You're right. So what do I do while waiting for divine intervention?"

"What you always do. After all, you didn't kill Louisa."

"Okay. Thanks. That's what I'll do. Greater is He that is within me, than he that is in the world."

"There you go. Feel better?"

Ember nodded.

Reece Sovern knocked at Harry's car window. Harry pressed a button and the window slid down.

"Good evening, Mr. Thurgood."

Harry nodded his response.

"We're through, Reverend."

"Did you find what you are looking for?" Ember asked.

"Can't officially say, and we still have your car to go over, but no we didn't. Of course, you didn't hear that from me." He turned to go away and then turned back to the car. "I'll give you a call when you can pick up your car."

"Thank you, Mr. Sovern."

"Sorry, for all of this. Just doing my job."

"We understand," Harry said.

"Goodnight." Sovern turned and left.

They watched him get into his car, and drive off.

Harry turned to Ember, and asked, "What say we get a bite to eat?"

"I don't think it's a good idea, Harry."

"Is there anything in your rulebook that says you can't eat supper with a man?"

"No, of course not. It's just that I don't want to give the gossips anymore reason to talk."

"Look, Em, if you don't give them something to talk about, they'll make it up, and that will be worse. Believe me. Just be yourself. It's just dinner. Silver Spoon?"

"I don't know why I'm letting you talk me into this, but okay. Not the Spoon, though. Let's go someplace out of town where there won't be any gawkers."

"Sounds good to me. I'll give you fifteen minutes to change."

"You really don't like black, do you?"

"Oh, I like black all right. Just not broadcloth or worsted wool."

Ember laughed, opened her car door, and said, "I'll be back."

***

They ended up at the Buttery Creek Beer Garden and Restaurant, a small microbrewery and eatery west of Llano.

On the way to the restaurant, Ember received a call from Effie Snyder, asking if she was okay. Ember assured her she was fine, and the call ended.

Harry had chuckled and made a comment about small towns and gossip.

After looking at the menu, she and Harry decided to get double orders of sausage and potato salad and a pitcher of a dark German-style beer.

While waiting for the food to arrive, Harry asked, "Does Effie call often?"

"Not really. But then I see her several times a week. She does a lot of work at the church. She's probably the one person in the church I could actually call a friend."

"That's good for you. I don't know her. What's she like?"

"She grew up here in town. Was friends with Louisa, but something happened there, and she started coming to my church. She can't stand Mary Lou." Ember gave a little laugh. "Effie is probably my staunchest supporter."

"Always good to have one of those."

"Yes, it is. She's one person I can always count on for help, too. She'll volunteer to do anything. And fills in for the receptionist. Carola's kids are always sick."

"Is Effie married?"

"No. A spinster, as they used to say and still do here. She was also an only child, and her parents apparently passed some years ago."

"That's too bad."

"It is kind of sad. I guess that's why she throws her heart and soul into the church. Chris Hayes said she was the same when she was at his church."

"Being a newbie, she probably doesn't have much clout, vis-a-vis Mary Lou."

"Not politically. But everyone seems to like her. She made a point to fit right in and she has. Why this interest in Effie?"

"Just curious. If we are to pull Mary Lou's teeth, it's good to know who can help us."

"Effie would do whatever she could to help. I just don't think she'll be much help in the end."

"That's okay. She's your friend, and that's what's most important."

The conversation drifted off to the advantages and disadvantages of pets, 80s versus 90s music, and whether or not electric cars would replace gasoline cars in the near future.

When they were finished eating, Harry drove back to Magnolia Bluff and dropped her off at the parsonage, wished her a good night, and drove off.

She watched until his taillights disappeared, then closed and locked her door. With hands on hips, she took in the mess that was her living room. Out from under the couch came Wilbur, and Ember scooped him up.

"If this is being careful, I'd hate to see them not being careful." She let out a big sigh and scratched under Wilbur's chin. "I'm not dealing with this tonight. Perhaps tomorrow, Effie will be able to help me get everything back the way it was."

Lying in bed, and before closing her eyes, the cat curled up on the pillow next to her, Ember said a prayer of thanks for Effie and Harry, and asked God to keep them both safe.

Chapter Twelve

TECHNICALLY DAWN, THE SKY was still dark as night. Miguel was busy when the buzzer sounded for the back door, so Harry went to see who was there.

He flipped on the back light, and opened the door. The face smiling at him was that of John Paul, Elder Smythe's handyman.

"Heard you were sick," Harry said.

"Oh, yes, sir. I was. But I'm all better now."

"Glad to hear it."

"I'm early because I have a special errand I have to run this morning. And I don't want to be late with my regulars. Hope you don't mind."

"Nope. Very considerate of you. Did you get everything on my order?"

"Everything but one item, Mr. Thurgood." John Paul took out a slip of paper. He looked at it, then showed it to Harry. "That circled word. I can't ever get that word."

"Arugula?"

"Yeah. That one. Elder Smythe said it will be ready next week."

"Okay. Everything else good?"

"Yes, sir. I'll get it for you."

John Paul loaded up the two-wheeler with a half-dozen boxes and wheeled it into the kitchen. He gave Harry the invoice and returned to the truck to put the two-wheeler away.

Harry came back out and gave John Paul a fifty dollar bill. "Do you have change?"

"I think so." The young man rummaged in the bank bag. "Is it three dollars?"

"No. Two dollars and fifty-three cents."

"Let's see." He paused, then asked, "Is that two quarters and three pennies?"

"Yes, it is. Plus two one dollar bills."

John Paul handed Harry the change. "Thank you, Mr Thurgood. Have a good day."

"Thanks. You, too, John Paul."

Harry watched him drive away, and found himself wondering once again who the young man reminded him of.

***

Mary Lou Fight did not have good thoughts towards Jasper Porter. Nine o'clock on a Friday morning was not a civil time to schedule a committee meeting.

She drove her Lincoln to the city hall, parked along the street, and got out of the car. She ran her hands down her dress, pressed the fob button to lock the car, and began walking.

Someone yelled, "Look out!"

Mary Lou turned her head to see who was yelling, felt something slam into her, and then she was falling. For a long time she fell before she was swallowed up by a pool as black as Texas oil.

***

Back in his office, Detective Reece Sovern pushed his glasses up and looked over his notes. Three people had seen the hit and run. No one had been able to catch the license plate number, and the three didn't agree on make or model of the vehicle. They did agree that the car was a dark color. But whether it was black, navy blue, brown, or gray, not one of the three could say.

The vehicle seemed to come out of nowhere, hit Mary Lou as she began walking away from her car, and kept on going. Which told Sovern that the hit was probably intentional, rather than accidental.

He would have loved to talk to her, but at this point Mary Lou was in a coma and not talking to anybody.

"That's the second Crimson Hat Society member in as many days," he muttered. "Which is just a bit too coincidental for my liking."

Aside from Mary Lou's group, what did the two women have in common?

The cigar rolled from one corner of his mouth to the other. "From the looks of it, that's all they had in common," he said to his desk.

He looked at the ceiling and frowned. There was all the gossip flying around town concerning Mary Lou and Reverend Cole, which gave Ember Cole a motive. After all, Mary Lou was threatening to get her canned from the church. At least that is what Ray Holden said, and he should know. He was after all the chairman of the pastor-parish relations committee.

Plenty of motive to kill someone who was threatening to destroy your career. And, sad to say, ministers weren't exempt from the baser human passions.

With the reverend's car at the garage and the forensics people crawling all over it, he'd know soon enough if her car was the one that had done in the Middlebrook woman.

His gaze shifted back to his notes. Unless Cole had gotten a car from someplace else or borrowed one from someone, she was off the hook for Mary Lou Fight. Unless she'd paid someone to do it. And that was a distinct possibility. In fact, it made a whole heck of a lot of sense to Sovern.

Then there was Harry Thurgood. "Now that's a guy with a past if I ever saw one," he muttered. "And he seems to be pretty thick with the Reverend. The gossips can't miss an unmarried man and a single woman spending time together. Which means they might be in it together. Maybe I should take a look at Thurgood's car. Although he seems too shrewd to use his own vehicle for something like this."

Sovern took the cigar out of his mouth, looked at the soggy end, pitched it towards the wastebasket, missed, and took a fresh stogie from his desk drawer to replace it.

He leaned back in his desk chair, cigar jutting out of his mouth, hands behind his head, and said to the ceiling, "Don't see sufficient motive to pin this on the Reverend or Thurgood. Maybe in time, but not right now." He sat up. "But somebody had sufficient motive, and if it isn't Cole or Thurgood, who is it? Then there's that nutty hat group. Other than the society, what connects Fight and Middlebrook? Or is that it?"

He shook his head and stood. He had more people to interview, and that wasn't going to happen sitting at his desk.

***

His early morning customers were gone by nine, and the coffee shop was empty. A total of five paying customers, including Ember, had passed through Harry's door.

He told Ember he thought she should probably get in touch with a lawyer, but she told him she would cross that bridge if she needed to.

Harry took advantage of the lull and called a lawyer he knew up in Dallas to find out if there was anyone good in Magnolia Bluff who could represent Ember should she need to have legal counsel. Twenty minutes later, he got a recommendation. Harry then called Stanton Mirabeau Lauderbach. And that's when he heard, courtesy of Lauderbach's receptionist, about the hit and run involving Mary Lou.

Harry smiled and thought, *Payback's always a bitch.*

As for Ember, Lauderbach agreed to help the Reverend should she need his services and would bill Harry. He also agreed not to mention who was paying his fee.

With that business taken care of, Harry retired to his corner table with a cup of pure Kona coffee and a doughnut.

With this latest development, he wondered if it was likely that Sovern would change his mind about Ember. Thus far his inquiry was just routine, and he'd told Ember as much. But with the attempt on Mary Lou, the police investigator just might want to seriously keep the crosshairs on Em.

Harry drank coffee. He took his pipe out of his pocket, and since no one was in the shop, filled it, and lit it. He puffed on the sweet Virginia blend, drank more coffee, and considered the options to get Sovern to shift his focus.

By the time the coffee cup was empty and the bowl of tobacco was half gone, he'd made up his mind. There was only one course of action they could take: the two of them had to find out who killed Louisa Middlebrook and made the attempt on Mary Lou, and then give the evidence to Sovern.

That was the only way to get the focus off Ember. Because Harry knew only too well that, being bureaucrats, the police would go for the easy arrest. And at this point in time, Ember was the easy arrest. And once arrested, they'd make sure the evidence fit the crime with the person they'd arrested.

"I think I'll wander over to the *Chronicle*. Neal ought to be able to give me the scoop. Although I could just as well stand on the street corner, because I bet everybody is talking."

Chapter Thirteen

JESSAMINE WALTER SAID GOODBYE to Betty Sue Fernhope and ended the call. Before Betty Sue, she'd gotten calls from Charmaine Adler, Terresa Brown, and Magnolia Nadine. The latter asking about membership in the Crimson Hat Society.

She absentmindedly kissed her husband goodbye.

"Don't wait on me for supper," he said. "I have a feeling this meeting will run overtime. These departmental budget meetings always do."

She nodded and smiled at him and went back to ruminating over the news. Mary Lou Fight in a coma. Mary Lou fighting for her life. Jessamine chuckled.

"Try talking your way out of this one, Mary Lou," she said to the empty dining room.

She poured herself a fresh cup of coffee, took the cup to the wet bar in the living room, and added a dollop of good Kentucky bourbon.

Jessamine sat in her favorite chair, a custom made Richmond by Saalfield and Beckman, and put her feet up on the ottoman. She sipped her coffee.

How convenient, she thought. *Without doing a thing, I may be able to become Queen of the society. Thank you, you wonderful person. Whoever you are.*

A smile spread across her face, and she took a deep sniff of the dark liquid.

"Oh, I do love a good cup of coffee," she said, and sipped.

She leaned her head back against the chair and thought of the calls she'd received earlier, particularly the one from Magnolia Nadine.

"Of all the nerve. To actually ask about membership in the Crimson Hat Society."

Jessamine sniffed her disdain, and drank coffee. "These upstarts. Always trying to become somebody."

She thought of Charleston. She thought of her roots.

"The Middletons and Chestnuts were people of importance long before there even was a Texas. My people served proudly in the War of Northern Aggression. And served the people of South Carolina after the carpetbaggers left."

Jessamine drank coffee. "I wonder what Magnolia Nadine writes down in that little book of hers? Could it be something juicy?" She sipped coffee. "If Mary Lou lives, she'll probably be out of commission for a long time. All the more reason for me to become queen. And if I were queen, I'd make sure we extended membership to those who'd be grateful for the recognition. And *not* grateful to Mary Lou."

She drank coffee. "Magnolia Nadine. Now she'd be grateful for the recognition. She'd probably see being a member of the society as a benefit to all of her do gooder activities. And—" A big smile appeared on Jessamine's face. "She'd probably do her best to make sure the Crimson Hat Society was very organized and efficient. Not just Mary Lou's toy. And that would irk Mary Lou to no end. In fact she just may try to take control of the group away from Mary Lou. To make it more efficient."

Coffee cup empty, Jessamine got a refill, and returned to her chair. "Yes. Magnolia might be a very good addition. Right after we bring in Ember Cole."

***

Crossing the green, on his way to the office of the *Magnolia Bluff Chronicle*, Harry spied Fergus sitting on a bench. The old drunk was eating a sausage. Harry had given the old guy enough pancakes, hashbrowns, and sausages for three, and boxed up what he hadn't eaten so Fergus could have something to eat later in the day.

"Hello, Fergus," Harry called out.

The old guy looked up, squinted, and nodded. Harry walked over to him. Fergus eyed him warily.

"Just want to chat a minute." Harry sat on the far end of the bench. As much to give the guy space as to stay upwind from his smell.

"Have a place to sleep tonight?"

Fergus shook his head.

Harry reached into his coat pocket and took out a pen and a business card. On the back of the card, he wrote a note, and then reached over, and held out the card to him.

"Take this, and give it to whoever's at the desk at the Cozy Corner's Motel tonight. Okay? It's going to be cold and I don't want you getting sick. And while you're there you can take a nice hot bath or shower. Make you feel like a million bucks."

Fergus took the card. "Thank you, Mr. Thurgood."

"Harry. Call me Harry."

Fergus smiled. "Okay, Harry."

By tomorrow, or probably sooner, Harry knew Fergus wouldn't remember. Didn't matter, though. It was a ritual, and there was a certain comfort in rituals.

"Awfully cold for May, isn't it, Mr. Thurgood."

"May? This is January."

"No, sir. Murders. We have murders in May. Not January. One every May. We had a murder. So this is May."

"Makes sense," Harry said. "Know anything about it?"

"Bad blood."

"What do you mean?"

"That woman died of bad blood."

"She was poisoned?"

Fergus shook his head. "Bad blood." He put the sausage in his mouth, and smacked his two fists together."

Harry nodded. "Where did you hear that?"

"Everywhere. It's on the wind. Whispers on the wind."

"Huh. Guess I better pay closer attention to what's blowing in the wind."

"Yes, sir."

"Thanks, Fergus. Don't forget the Cozy Corners tonight. You don't want to be out in the cold."

"No, sir."

Harry stood, and continued on his walk to the *Chronicle*.

When he crossed the sill, he saw Rebecca at her desk. "Hello, Rebecca. How are you this fine morning?"

"I'm doing just peachy, Harry. What brings you here? Looking to run another ad?"

"As if that would do any good. No, I want to talk with Neal."

"As you can see, our resident curmudgeon is at his desk."

Harry tipped his hat to her and walked over to Neal's desk.
"Hey, Neal, how are things?"

Neal Holland looked up from the sheet of paper on his desk. "Things are good, Harry. Got a murder and an attempted murder of none other than Mary Lou Fight. That'll sell more papers than a win by the high school football team or if the Primitive Baptists bought an organ. Maybe more than if the mayor ran off with the sheriff."

Harry laughed. "I dunno. That last one might sell a lot of papers."

With a twinkle in his eye, Neal admitted it just might at that.

"So what can I do for you?" The newspaper man leaned back in his chair and put his hands behind his head.

"What do you know about Louisa and Mary Lou?"

"Louisa is dead and Mary Lou's in a coma."

"That's it?"

"As far as anything definite, that's it. Sovern is keeping the details close to his chest."

"Do you know how Louisa died?"

"According to the JP, someone whacked her pretty hard on the head. Then laid her out on the ground and drove a car over her. Maybe a pickup. Then dumped her body in the cemetery."

"And no one saw anything?"

"Not that Sovern is saying, and not that I've been able to find out."

"Doesn't it seem odd that no one saw anything?"

"Maybe. Then again, people do have to sleep sometime. Not many choose to sleep down by the cemetery either."

Harry nodded, took his hat off, and set in on the edge of Neal's desk. "It couldn't have been a pretty sight for those kids to come across."

"No, it wasn't. Husband's pretty broken up about it. Second marriage for both, and, according to him, she was the one."

"That's rough."

"That it is." Neal sat up and folded his hands on his desk. "So what's your interest in all of this?"

"Because of some gossip, I think Sovern might start focusing on Reverend Cole."

"Uh-huh. Well, it isn't just Reverend Cole you should be thinking about."

"What do you mean?"

"Hear tell that Sovern has you in his sights as well. After all, it's no secret you're rather chummy with the Reverend."

"We're friends."

Neal shrugged. "No business of mine."

Harry barked a laugh. "Everything's your business, Neal."

A faint smile touched the newspaperman's lips. "Okay. You got me there."

"So what's the scuttlebutt?"

"Nothing definite. Just that the two of you are pals, and that maybe you're in on this together. And if the gossips are driving down that road, you know Sovern is too."

Harry didn't like this piece of information one bit. If Sovern started digging into his past… Well, that just wasn't something Harry could allow to happen.

To steer Neal in a different direction, he asked, "Was Louisa well liked?"

"I'd say generally so. She was a member of Mary Lou's group and that can bring its own problems."

"How so?"

"Mary Lou makes demands, and sometimes they're pretty tough."

"In what way?"

"Like initiation rites. Take Betty Sue Fernhope for example. I think she and Stanley were members of the Church of Christ. But for Betty Sue to be in the Crimson Hat Society she had to join the Methodist Church."

"You're kidding."

"No, I'm not."

"That's downright mean."

"Won't argue with that. For Mary Lou, it's a test of loyalty. With Louisa, I heard tell that she had to give up all of her old friends. Caused a big rift between her and Effie Snyder to the point where Effie left the Baptist Church and joined the Methodist."

"But that's where Mary Lou goes."

Neal shrugged.

For a moment, Harry stared off into space, then said, "That would explain why Effie hates Mary Lou and is such a staunch supporter of Ember."

"I suppose so."

"What do you know about Mary Lou's hit and run?"

"Not much. Car comes out of nowhere, hits her, and doesn't stop."

"No details?"

"People are very unobservant, Harry. Stand on the street corner, then ask the passersby if they even saw you. If they did, ask them the color of your suit. You'll get ten different answers from as many people, if they even recall you were wearing a suit. Which makes gossips like Mary Lou so deadly — she sees and remembers *everything*."

"Very true. So no leads for Sovern to follow up on?"

"At least none he is willing to share." Neal leaned back in his chair and put his hands behind his head.

"So tell me, Harry, why you're concerned about this. It isn't all just about Ember Cole, is it?"

A smile touched Harry's lips. *Neal doesn't miss a damn thing.* To the newspaperman, he said, "Look, Ember's young and I'm just trying to help. Sure, I don't want Reece poking around in my business, but I can handle him. Ember, on the other hand, is like a chocolate bar in your car window on a sunny August day."

"I think she has more savvy than you give her credit for. You sure you aren't looking for a damsel to rescue?"

Harry laughed. "I plead the fifth."

"Thought so." Neal stood. "Tell you what. Let me know if you find out something, and I'll do likewise."

Harry stood, stuck out his hand, said, "Deal," and they shook hands on it.

***

Neal watched Harry Thurgood leave. When the door had closed behind him, Neal took a plain brown envelope out of his desk drawer, and a plain manilla folder out of the envelope.

A sticky note on the folder informed him that the contents were a copy of the initial police report. He opened the folder and began reading the first sheet of paper.

In the back of his mind, he thought, *Sources. Where would a newspaperman be without them?*

Chapter Fourteen

Reece Sovern had just finished talking to Gunter Fight, and was standing on the sidewalk in front of the bank. The most interesting piece of information that Gunter had provided was the little tidbit that Thurgood had threatened his wife.

The police investigator saw Harry Thurgood leave the newspaper office. *I wonder what Thurgood was doing at the* Chronicle*?*

He watched him cross West Main Street, trot across the green, cross East Main, and enter the coffee shop. The detective thought a moment, decided now was as good a time as any, and in a minute was crossing Main Street and entering the Really Good.

Harry looked up from where he was standing behind the counter and said, "Hello, Detective. Coffee?"

Sovern hesitated, and Harry added, "On the house."

"Sure, why not?" The police investigator walked up to the counter. Harry set a cup of coffee in front of him.

"Is there someplace we can talk, Thurgood?"

"That table in the corner. I'll join you in a second."

Sovern walked to the table, sat, and in a moment Harry joined him.

"So what's on your mind, Detective?"

"This is really good coffee. Sure beats the heck out of the grocery store stuff."

"It's Celebes Kalossi, grown on the island of Sulawesi in Indonesia. It'll only set you back seventeen bucks for a pound."

"Seventeen? That's a bit rich for my wallet. But thank you for the experience." He took a sip, then asked, "Where you from, Harry?"

"Up north."

Sovern nodded. *Yep. Somewhere up north, and probably not New England or New York.* "Care to be more specific?"

"No."

Sovern nodded and took a sip of coffee. "S'pose you heard someone did a hit and run on Mary Lou Fight this morning."

"I heard. The one thing this town doesn't lack is a gossip hotline."

Sovern nodded.

"Close to nine, wasn't it?" Harry said.

"Uh-huh. Where were you around then?"

"Here. You can ask Miguel."

"I'm sure I can, and I'm sure he'll corroborate your story." Sovern drank coffee. "You pay him very well from what I hear."

"I pay him a livable wage so he can support his family. And he works hard for the money."

"I'm sure he does. Probably pretty loyal, too, I bet."

"What's that supposed to mean?"

"Just sayin'." Sovern finished his coffee.

"A refill?"

"No, I'm good. Thanks. Was Reverend Cole here around nine?"

"Not sure. She might have left by then."

"I hear tell that the Reverend is none too popular with Mary Lou and her circle."

"Don't know where you heard that."

"So they're all best of friends?"

"Didn't say that."

"Does the Reverend have a temper?"

"Not that I've seen."

Sovern nodded.

The door opened and in walked Scarlett Hayden. She was wearing a red ankle-length dress, with long sleeves, belted at the waist with a gold chain, and a neckline that plunged to the waist.

Sovern glanced in her direction, and muttered, "Jesus H Christ."

A smirk played on Harry's lips. "She likes attention," he said confidentially.

Sovern shook his head.

"Anything else, Detective?"

"No. Don't want to take you from your customer. Hear tell you don't have many."

"Starting a business is tough, even in the best economic climate."

"Thanks for the coffee."

"Anytime."

Sovern left the shop and stood on the sidewalk looking up and down the street. He took a cigar out of his pocket, removed the cellophane, and stuck it in his mouth.

Probably should check in with Reverend Cole, he thought, and turned south towards Church Street.

Wonder if she knows anything about Thurgood's visit with Mary Lou and him threatening her?

Chapter Fifteen

EMBER COLE HAD BEEN seated at her desk in the church office no more than five minutes when Reece Sovern knocked on the doorframe.

She looked up and said, "Good morning, Mr. Sovern. How may I help you?"

"Hello, Ms. Cole. Do you have time to answer a few questions?"

"I do. Please have a seat."

Ember remained at her desk, and Sovern sat in one of the two chairs on the other side. She folded her hands on her desk blotter, said a silent prayer, and waited for the detective to speak.

He took a notebook out of his pocket, thumbed through it, until he found the page he was looking for. After a moment, he looked at Ember.

"I suppose you heard about Mary Lou Fight."

"Yes. I got a call from Janet Priestly shortly after nine. Do you know the Priestlys?"

"Enough to say, 'Hello, how are you?' What were you doing when you got the call from Mrs. Priestly?"

"I was putting my home back together from your carefully performed search."

A faint smile appeared on Sovern's lips, and just as quickly it disappeared. "Can anyone verify that?"

"Wilbur."

"Who's Wilber?"

"My cat."

Sovern chuckled and shook his head. "Nice. Can any human verify you were home?"

"No. I didn't know I'd be needing a witness."

"I'm just doing my job, Reverend Cole. We don't need to be adversaries."

"At least not until you arrest me."

"Well, maybe we ought to cross that bridge when we come to it."

There was a knock, and a man stuck his head in. Sovern turned around and said, "What are you doing here, Stanton?"

"I'm here to talk to Reverend Cole. I'm her legal counsel."

"You're what?" Sovern demanded.

"I didn't hire you," Ember said.

"No, you didn't, Ms. Cole. A friend hired me on your behalf in case you needed legal advice." Stanton Lauderbach nodded towards Sovern, to emphasize his point, and continued, "Stanton Lauderbach, Esquire at your service, and it looks as though I got here just in time."

"Look Stanton, the Reverend and I are just having a chat. I'm not arresting her."

"But she is a person of interest. Is she not?"

Reece Sovern took his glasses off and ran his hand over his face. "Yes, the Reverend is a person of interest."

"Then I arrived just in time." Lauderbach sat in the chair next to Sovern. "Continue, Reece."

Sovern put his glasses back on, took in a deep breath, and exhaled. "Ms. Cole, did you know that your friend, Harry Thurgood, paid Mary Lou Fight a visit yesterday, and, according to her husband, threatened her?"

Lauderbach held up his hand to stop Ember from replying. "And what does that have to do with Ms. Cole? Shouldn't you be discussing Mr. Thurgood's alleged threat with him?"

Ember looked from Sovern, to the lawyer, and then back to the police investigator.

Sovern stood. "You want to make this difficult, don't you, Stanton?"

"Just doing my job."

"Yeah, right. Well, I'll leave you two to whatever business you have. Ms. Cole. Stanton."

The police investigator left, and Ember took in the man sitting before her. He was immaculately dressed in a three-piece charcoal gray suit. His dark hair was combed straight back from his high forehead, but stood out from his head, giving a very full appearance. He had an aquiline nose and thin lips. But what she found most impressive were his piercing, almost feral eyes. And his smile: genuine, but rather too genuine.

"Who hired you?"

"I'm not at liberty to say."

"Really?"

"That was the condition your benefactor put on the arrangement."

"I see. Why are you here?"

"To meet you and find out what Detective Sovern has asked you thus far."

"And if I say no to your services?"

"If I may be direct..."

Ember nodded.

"You'd be a fool to do so. I'm the best in the county at this sort of thing."

"Modest, aren't we?"

Lauderbach smiled. "No, I'm not. But I am the best, which is why Sovern left. He was fishing. Which is good for him and bad for you. He has no evidence you are involved. Let him come back when he has some. Now, what has he asked you about?"

Ember filled in the attorney on her interactions with Reece Sovern.

When she was finished, Stanton Lauderbach fished a card out of his suit coat pocket and handed it to her. He stood. "Call me, no matter the time, whenever someone official shows up."

"Aren't you going to ask if I'm innocent?"

Lauderbach smiled, and Ember could've sworn his eyes glowed. "My job is to defend you. Period. Guilt or innocence is up to judge and jury. Good day, Reverend Cole."

Ember watched him leave, and then studied the chair in which he'd been sitting. She pursed her lips, then picked up her desk phone. "This is Harry's doing," she muttered, started punching in numbers, but stopped before she was finished.

Her eyes took in her Bible, and she returned the phone to the cradle. She mouthed the verse: *Be welcoming to strangers; because, by doing so, some have entertained angels and didn't realize it.*

She sat back in her chair, and softly said, "Maybe Harry is an angel."

Chapter Sixteen

HARRY THURGOOD WAS BUSY. There were ten people eating lunch in his coffee shop. He went from table to table as a bumblebee traveled from flower to flower.

The snippets of conversation he managed to pick up reinforced his suspicion that gossip was flying around town about Ember and him and the Hats. People, being the snoops they are, were checking him out.

He didn't mind. Let them check all they wanted, as long as they bought lunch while doing so. Let the road to their satisfaction be paved in green.

When Ember Cole walked through the door, Harry knew it, because all conversation stopped for just a moment. This is what they had been waiting for.

She smiled, waved, and said a few words to those folks she knew as she made her way to a stool at the far end of the counter. Once seated, she took off her hat, and grabbed a menu from the holder on the counter, and perused her options even though she didn't need to.

Harry handed an order to Miguel and walked behind the long counter to stand opposite of her.

"What's going on?" she asked. "I've never seen you this busy."

"That's because I've never been this busy. What will you have?"

"Are you an angel?"

"My mother thought so."

"I suppose, if you were, you wouldn't tell me."

"Are you serious?"

"Yes."

"You want to know if I have wings, wear white, and fly around when I'm not working here?"

"Now you're making fun of me."

"Sorry, Em, I didn't mean to. I get it. You believe in angels."

She nodded.

"You've known me for, what, three years?"

She nodded again.

"Doesn't that answer your question?"

"Why are you so good to me?"

"What do you mean?"

"Lauderbach. That was you." She held up her hand. "Don't deny it, mister. If you aren't an angel, and I wouldn't expect you to admit it if you were, but if you aren't, why are you so nice to me?"

"Hold that thought. I'm being waved at."

Harry departed, and after taking care of the couple's payment for the lunch and encouraging them to stop in again, he returned to Ember.

"Okay. You want to know why I'm nice to you?"

"Yes, I do."

"Because, Ember Cole, I really, really like you. That's why."

She held her lower lip between her teeth, eyes focused on the menu. Her cheeks turned red.

Harry continued. "Besides, like I said, my mother thought I was an angel..." She looked at him, and he winked at her. "So maybe I am."

"You are incorrigible, Mr. Thurgood." A smile spread across her face.

"I know it, and you love it. Now, what will you have?"

"My usual."

"One usual coming right up."

***

Four more people came in for lunch, which kept Harry sufficiently busy that he couldn't chat to any great length with Ember.

When she left, he returned her wave goodbye, his eyes holding hers long enough that someone in the coffee shop probably noticed, but he didn't care. She was beautiful and he didn't want to stop looking.

The time was close to two when the last customer left.

Miguel surveyed the empty shop from the kitchen window. "Today was a good day, Mr. Thurgood. Maybe your luck has changed."

"Maybe, Miguel. Maybe it has at that."

"What do you want me to make for your supper?"

"That's okay. I think I'll grab a pizza at Olivia's."

"Si, Mr. Thurgood. She makes good pizza."

"That she does."

Harry and Miguel finished cleaning up for the day, and at three Harry flipped the sign from open to closed and locked the door. Miguel said goodbye, and Harry took a cup of coffee and a slice of apple pie to his corner table.

He took a bite of pie and marveled at how delicious it was. *God bless Noonan*, he thought. *Where would this town be without Bluff Bakery*.

Harry ate another forkful of pie, drank coffee, and retrieved his phone from his suit coat pocket, telling it to call Lauderbach. When the lawyer finally answered, Harry asked him how things were with Ember.

"I think she'll be just fine, as long as she doesn't talk with anyone official. Unless I'm there, of course."

"That's good to hear. You've spoken with her, then?"

"Oh, yes. Got there just in time. Sovern was on a fishing expedition. And we don't want the Reverend helping to bait the hook."

"No, we don't want that."

"I told her as much, and I think she got the picture."

"That's good."

"Yes, it is. Also, just so you know, Sovern knows about your visit to Mary Lou Fight. He was asking the Reverend about it."

"Really?"

"Yes, sir."

"Thanks, Stanton, for letting me know and for helping Ember."

"My pleasure, Harry."

The call ended, and Harry put a piece of pie in his mouth, slowly savoring it before swallowing. He held up another piece and spoke. "So Sovern knows about my visit to Mary Lou. I wonder why he didn't ask me about it? Why ask Ember?" The piece of pie made its way to his mouth.

He chewed and swallowed. *Must be saving it for... For what?* He lifted the coffee cup. "I have no idea. No idea at all." He drank coffee, put the cup down, and continued his musing, “Maybe I should ask Sovern, so this can be put to rest. Then again, maybe I should let him work for it.”

Chapter Seventeen

REECE SOVERN WAS PISSED. Of all the rotten luck. Someone had hired Lauderbach to represent Reverend Cole. He took a bite of his burger, chewed, and swallowed. That lawyer was going to make this case a whole lot more difficult. And that he didn't need.

For now, he'd set Ember Cole aside and focus on Thurgood and the Crimson Hat brigade.

He took a bite of burger and followed it with a gulp of Orange Crush. *I should probably talk to the remaining Crimson Hat gals this afternoon,* he thought, *and save Thurgood for tonight.*

He stuck a French fry in his mouth and chewed while watching Betty Sue and Stanley Fernhope make their way to a table. "Speak of the devil," he muttered.

Sovern watched the couple while he ate. Betty Sue was excited over something, because she was talking quite fast, her face was intense, and her hands emphasized everything she said. Stanley just stared at his napkin.

Interesting, Sovern thought. He'd talk to them later. Let them eat in peace, or as much peace as they could, given how upset Betty Sue seemed to be.

He finished his lunch, dropped thirteen dollars next to his plate to cover meal and tip, and left the Silver Spoon.

Standing on the sidewalk, he unwrapped a cigar, stuck it in his mouth, and walked back to the city hall and police complex to get his car. He'd start by talking to Scarlett Hayden.

***

Sovern drove around the north end of Burnet Reservoir to Hayden's Resort, which was situated on the northwest shore of the reservoir.

He remembered when the Haydens had bought the fifty acres, put in twenty cabins, and then added a campground with twenty spots. They'd built a fabulous Prairie-style home for themselves, as well.

After all these years, the whole shebang must be worth a few millions, the detective thought, as he pulled into the drive, which was marked private. He wound his way through bald cypress, pecan, Texas ash, cottonwood, bur oak, and cedar elm. He emerged in a clearing. He recognized Scarlett's big Land Rover and speculated that the beat up Honda parked next to it belonged to some young guy from the college. If one were to believe the gossip, that is.

Of course, if one did believe the gossip, Scarlett Hayden would rarely, if ever, be vertical. And he'd just seen her a little while ago in a vertical position. Besides, she had a resort to run, even though the Smiths did much of the day to day management, Scarlett still had to watch the big picture, which probably meant she was vertical quite a bit of the time.

He parked his car, got out, and walked up to the door. A vision flashed before his eyes of Scarlett walking into Thurgood's coffee shop. He shook his head and pressed the doorbell.

After what seemed forever, the door opened.

"Mr. Sovern. What a pleasant surprise. What can I do for you?"

She was wearing one of those filmy white outfits that women wore in the movies from the 1930s. *Jesus*, he said to himself. Out loud he said, "I'd like to ask you a few questions."

"Sure. C'mon in." She stepped away from the door and headed for somewhere in the house.

He entered, closed the door, and followed. Her outfit billowed behind her like a cumulus cloud until she stopped at a door.

"We can talk in here." Her hand motioned for Sovern to enter the room, which he did.

Scarlett followed and sat on the sofa, then tucked her legs under her.

Sovern sat, met her gaze, swallowed, pushed his glasses up his nose, and asked, "What happens if Mary Lou dies? With the society, that is?"

"We elect a new queen. And we'll add a couple new members."

"What does the society actually do?"

Scarlett chuckled. "It doesn't *do* anything, Mr. Sovern. We girls just wanna have fun. So, we have fun."

"I find it difficult to picture Mary Lou Fight having fun."

Scarlett laughed loudly. "Then you don't know Mary Lou. She has the most fun of us all. All of her gossipy little doings. She damn well has everyone in fear of her. What will she tell? What will she not? And at what price?"

"And you? Does she have you in the palm of her hand?"

"Good lord, no. But that's only because I don't give a damn."

"So who do you think would want Louisa Middlebrook and Mary Lou Fight dead?"

"Louisa?" Sovern watched her cock her head and aim her eyes at the ceiling, and hold that pose for a moment, before turning those dark orbs of hers back to him. "I don't have a clue. Most likely someone she pissed off when she became Mary Lou's lap dog."

"Lap dog?"

"Oh, yes. Mary Lou gave Louisa social standing. Made her somebody. And for that honor, she practically worshipped Mary Lou."

Sovern thought on that for a moment, and then said, "And Mrs. Fight?"

Once again, Scarlett's throaty laugh filled the room. "You'd be better off asking, Reece..."

The investigator couldn't help but notice how she drew out his name and that her eyes became filled with longing. He cleared his throat.

"You'd be better off asking who didn't want to kill her."

"And who might that be?"

"I'd guess her husband, Harry Thurgood, and myself, of course. Actually, I have second thoughts about her husband."

"Why do you exempt Thurgood and yourself?"

"Because neither one of us gives a damn about this little pimple on the butt of nowhere."

***

The sun sat low on the western horizon. A call to her husband confirmed he would be home late.

"Just saw the agenda for the meeting," he said. "It's going to be a long one. I'll get supper when I get home."

A smile appeared on Jessamine's face. *Of course you will*, she mused. *Right after you've finished getting your rocks off with some busty bimbo of a student.*

She ended the call with hubby and immediately dialed Terrell's number. "I have a project for you. Can you come over right now?"

"Uh, sure thing Mrs. Walter. Gimme half an hour."

Jessamine ended the call, and went to her bedroom. She removed her clothes and slipped on the black negligee. It had been a long time since she'd worn it, but it still fit.

"Watching one's weight does pay dividends."

She walked down to the living room and took a seat.

That boy is so muscular, so powerful, she mused. She liked the thought of him dominating her. Sometimes it was fun being on the receiving end.

The doorbell rang. She crossed the room to the door, peered through the peephole, and then opened the door.

At first a look of surprised crossed Terrell's face, and then a smile broke out on his lips. "Hello, Mrs. Walter."

"I thought we could have a little pleasure before business."

Chapter Eighteen

HARRY THURGOOD SAT IN a corner booth and took in the sight and smell of his pepperoni, mushroom, and anchovy pizza, and the aroma was heavenly. He took a sip of his Texas Gewürztraminer, set down the glass, and reached for a slice of pizza, when a shadow fell across the table.

He looked up. "Scarlett. To what do I owe the honor?"

She sat across from him. Her very long and very dark hair was done up in two loose braids that came together in a bun at the back of her head. She had changed from the nothing-left-to-the-imagination dress he'd seen her in earlier, to a simple blouse, jacket, and long, full skirt.

"Reece came to see me today."

"I'm not surprised. He's probably going to talk to half the town."

She picked up a slice of pizza, started to take a bite, and stopped. "You put those smelly fish on your pizza? Ugh." She put the slice down.

A smile barely lifted the corners of Harry's lips. "Sorry. If I'd known you were coming, I'd have left them off."

"Uh-huh. And white wine with pizza? God, Harry, I thought you were a connoisseur."

"It's Gewürztraminer. I like it's spiciness as a counterfoil to all the salt."

"Sure. Whatever you say."

"So, what did Reece ask you?"

She told him and flagged a waitress. "Red wine," she said to the young woman.

"I find that amusing," he said.

"What?"

"That we didn't kill Louisa or rundown Mary Lou because we don't give a damn about this pimple on the backside of nowhere."

"It's true, isn't it?"

Scarlett's wine arrived, and she swallowed a mouthful.

"True enough," Harry agreed.

"You know, I make a pretty good pizza. Lasagna, too, if you're interested."

"Do you have Gewürtz?"

"I can get some."

When Harry didn't say anything, she finished her wine in two gulps, stood, and said, "Think about it. Bye, Harry."

"See ya around, Scarlett."

He watched her leave, and thought, *Of all the times and places to have someone like her throw herself at me.* He shook his head and chuckled. *Just my luck.*

"Well, Harry," he said, just under his breath, "at least you know where you stand with Ember and Scarlett. Now, if I could only pigeonhole Reece Sovern."

He finished his pizza and wine, paid the bill, and walked the three blocks back to his place. As he unlocked the door to the stairs that led up to his flat above the coffee shop, a car door opened, and he heard the voice of Reece Sovern.

"Evening, Harry."

"What can I do for you, Reece?"

"Answer a few questions."

"Sure. Come on up."

Harry climbed the long flight of stairs to his flat, with the police investigator following. He unlocked the door, entered, and flipped a light switch. Sovern followed him in.

"Close the door, would you Reece? Something to drink?"

"Coke."

"By that, you Texans mean a soft drink. Am I right?"

"Yeah. What do you Yankees call it, soda?"

"Pop, where I'm from. All I have is ginger ale. Will that work?"

Sovern indicated it would. Harry filled a glass with ice cubes, added the ginger ale, and handed the glass to the investigator. For himself, he mixed a Corpse Reviver No. 1.

"What the hell is that you're drinking?" Sovern asked.

Harry told him.

"What's in it?"

"Cognac, Calvados, and sweet vermouth."

"Gimme a beer any day."

Harry smiled. "To each his own. So what do you want to ask me?"

"I spent the afternoon talking with Betty Sue Fernhope, Jessamine Walter, Charmaine Adler, and Scarlett Hayden."

"And what did the Hats tell you?"

"The same thing everyone else has: they have no idea who'd want to kill Louisa, and that people were waiting in line to knock off Mary Lou."

"Sounds about right."

Sovern took a big swallow of ginger ale. "The Hayden woman said something interesting." And he went on to tell Harry about Scarlett's opinion of Louisa.

"Interesting. You think there's something there?"

"What do you think?"

"I'd say it's worth checking out."

Sovern nodded, drank ginger ale, and said, "So why did you threaten Mary Lou?"

"Where did you hear that?"

"Gunter."

Harry nodded, sipped his drink, and said, "Makes sense he'd say something like that."

"Well, did you?"

"I quoted from *Messiah*."

"And?"

Harry repeated what he'd said to Mary Lou.

Sovern frowned. "Rather veiled."

"More like a statement of cause and effect. You attack the Lord's Anointed, don't expect him to sit back and do nothing."

"And are you the Lord's hammer?"

"Rod of iron, actually. And no, I'm not."

"The way I see it, Harry, is that Mary Lou goes on the warpath and decides she wants Reverend Cole out of the pulpit. But the Reverend doesn't want to leave. So she kills, or has someone kill Mary Lou's most ardent supporter, and when Mary Lou doesn't back down, she goes after Mary Lou."

"Interesting theory. I suppose you see me as Ember's cohort in crime."

"Something like that."

"Well, Reece, you're barking up the wrong tree."

"Am I? You threatened Mary Lou, and then she is rundown. That's quite a coincidence, and I don't believe in coincidences."

"I'd say that's your problem."

"Not if I make it yours."

Harry took a sip of his drink. "You can certainly try. But you're pissing into the wind if you do."

"We'll see about that." Sovern stood. "Goodnight, Thurgood."

Harry stood. "Goodnight, Detective."

Sovern left. Harry locked up for the night, returned to his chair, and sipped his drink.

"Things aren't looking too good for the home team." He said to the empty room. "Em and I need to find who killed Louisa and tried to kill Mary Lou, or else Lauderbach is going to be earning a lot more money."

Chapter Nineteen

SATURDAY MORNING FOUND REVEREND Ember Cole wishing she could go away with her friends. If she had any, that is.

She looked at Wilbur. "I shouldn't be so hard on myself, should I? After all, I have you." She reached down and picked up her cat. "And I have Effie and Harry.

Wilbur yawned and Ember set him on the floor. He immediately jumped up onto the bed and curled up into a ball on her pillow.

She thought of Harry. Her guardian angel. The first man she'd let get even somewhat close to her in a very long time. *But how long will he be interested if I don't...?* She left the thought hanging, finished dressing, told Wilbur goodbye, and walked out the front door. She locked it and set off for breakfast at the Really Good.

The quiet of the early morning was the best part of the day. Second best was the quiet of midnight and the very early hours of the morning. She prayed as she walked, reminding herself that God was her best friend. More faithful and constant than any human could ever be. And just about as difficult to understand sometimes. But whereas humans often did things out of confused purposes, God's purpose was steadfast. Even if we didn't always understand it.

And even though I walk through the valley of the shadow of death, you are with me, my Lord. You will never forsake me.

Fifteen minutes later, she was walking into Harry's coffee shop. She inhaled a deep lungful of the coffee aromas, intermingled with that of the hickory wood, the fresh aroma of cinnamon rolls, and that new blintz Harry was experimenting with.

She sat at the counter, removed her hat, and looked around. There wasn't a single soul in the place, except for Harry, Miguel, and herself. She wondered where Fergus was, and hoped he wasn't in jail.

Harry came out from the kitchen and walked to where she was sitting. "Just going over the delivery from John Paul. I don't know what it is about that young man, but I can't stop thinking I've seen him some place before."

"Can't help you there. Don't remember when the last time was that I saw him."

"Oh, well, I suppose it doesn't matter." He put his elbows on the counter, and gazed into Ember's face. "A good morning to you, Reverend Cole. And how are we this fine and chilly morning?"

She returned his smile. "Warmer, now that I'm here."

"Some coffee to further warm your bones?"

"Sure."

Harry poured coffee and lots of cream into a cup, dropped in two sugars, and set it before Ember with a spoon. She began stirring.

"I think I'm going to put that on the board as Reverend Cole's White Coffee."

"Don't you dare!"

"Why not? Don't you want to be famous?"

"That'll be the day."

"You'll make me cry."

Ember narrowed her eyes. "Is that another corny song reference?"

"All of life is a song."

She rolled her eyes.

"Anyway, just you wait. When I open branches in Austin and San Antonio, you'll see. You'll be famous. Like the colonel. Heck, I might even hire you."

"Get outta here." Ember took a sip of her coffee.

"On a more important note, we have to get serious about finding out who bumped off Louisa and tried to bump off Mary Lou."

"Why? What happened?"

"Sovern. That's what happened."

"What do you mean?"

"He found out I threatened, as he called it, Mary Lou and now both of us are in his crosshairs."

"Oh, dear."

"That's putting it rather delicately, but, yes, oh dear is right. We are in the hot water, missy."

"I guess you aren't an angel."

"What do you mean?"

"You're worried."

"Ah. Well, I could just be testing your faith."

"Yeah, right. Okay, Mister Angel, any suggestions where to start?"

"Yes. You talk to everybody. Make house calls. Ministers do that, so you won't raise any suspicions. While you're doing that, I'll be talking to a few select people. People who usually have their ear to the ground."

"Okay. Who's going to cover the shop while you're out nosing around?"

"I think I can get Miguel's cousin Estrelita to take care of the tables, he's waiting for her to reply to a text he sent her, and I left a message for old Jack Bonhoffer to see if he's willing to watch over things. He's retired and, from what I heard, ran a restaurant in Houston some years ago."

"Okay. I think we have ourselves a plan."

"At least it's a start. You want your usual?"

"You bet."

Chapter Twenty

THE FORENSICS REPORT ON Reverend Cole's car was sitting on his desk when he arrived. Sovern thumbed through it, found the conclusion, read it, and tossed the report back on to his desk.

"So the Reverend's car wasn't the one that crushed the life out of Louisa Middlebrook," he said out loud. "Damn, and double damn."

He got a cigar out of his desk drawer, removed the cellophane, stuck it in his mouth, got up, and began pacing back and forth in front of his desk.

"She has motive," he began. "What I am missing is means and opportunity. But if I can establish the means, I think opportunity will take care of itself."

He sat down at his desk and put his feet up on a corner.

"So, if she didn't use her car, she had to have used someone else's. That, or she had an accomplice. And her most likely accomplice is Thurgood."

He rolled the cigar to the other side of his mouth. "What I need is something that connects those two tighter than a child-proof cap to a bottle."

Sovern put his feet on the floor, stood, slipped on his overcoat, and walked out to his car. It was time for round two with the Crimson Hat Brigade.

***

Ember decided the first person she should talk to was Terresa Brown. She had a certain reputation, and not one that endeared her to many people.

She liked to pump you for information. And while she liked to get information, she wasn't too keen on giving any away. But on the off chance she might get lucky, Ember thought Terresa was worth a go.

She got her moped from the parsonage and rode it the eight blocks to Terresa Brown's place. She parked on the street in front of the house, walked up the walk, and rang the doorbell.

The door opened, and Ember was face to face with the squint-eyed, frowning, old sourpuss.

"Good morning, Ms. Brown. Lovely morning, isn't it?"

"Whatever you're selling, I'm not interested."

"I'm Ember Cole, pastor of the Methodist Church."

Terresa's eyes squinted more than usual, if that was even possible, and her face moved closer to Ember's.

"Oh, yes, I remember you. What do you want?"

"I'm just out talking to people. It's good to know your neighbors, don't you think?"

"I'm churched, you know."

"That I do. I'm not proselytizing. I'm just being neighborly. Are you busy?"

"Not particularly. Just having a second cup of coffee." Suddenly a smile appeared, not a large one, but it was a smile nonetheless. "Would you like coffee?"

"Sure."

"Come in."

Ember walked into the house, which to her eyes looked like way more house than a single person would need.

There was a small entryway and a hall that led to the back of the house. On the right, there was a door and stairs going up to the second floor. To the left, there were glass doors opening into the living room, and it was there that Terresa took her.

"Have a seat." Terresa indicated the sofa. "Do you take anything in your coffee?"

Ember sat. "Cream and sugar."

Terresa left the room and returned a couple minutes later with a tray of coffee paraphernalia, which she placed on the table that was between the sofa and the chair Terresa was using.

Ember doctored her coffee and took a sip. *Probably instant*, she thought.

Terresa squinted at her, and asked, "Is Mrs. Fight still alive?"

"The last I heard she was."

"I suppose it's difficult for you to minister to her, what with her trying to get you out of the church and all."

If Terresa knows that, Ember thought, *then the whole town knows it.* Out loud she said, "She's still one of my parishioners."

"Perhaps if you and Mr. Thurgood got married..."

"Married? We're just friends."

"I see."

"You mean people think that Harry, Mr. Thurgood, and I...?"

"People do talk, Reverend Cole, don't they?"

Ember drank coffee, before saying, "Yes, they do. What else are they saying?"

Terresa shrugged. "Heavens, if I know. It's not like I'm a busybody, like some people. I live alone and mind my own business. But I'd be careful about getting too close to Mr. Thurgood. I've heard he's running from the law. Some place up north wants him. Some sort of scam, I hear tell. Stole a lot of people's money."

"It's not true."

Terresa Brown shrugged. "You should know. Being friends and all."

Ember looked at her watch. "Goodness. I need to get going. Thank you for the coffee."

"Anytime, my dear."

Ember left, got on her moped, and drove back to the parsonage. And all the way home she asked herself what did she really know about Harry Thurgood?

Chapter Twenty-one

REECE SOVERN PARKED HIS car on the street in front of Stanley and Betty Sue Fernhope's home. He got out, walked up to the door, and rang the doorbell.

After a moment, the door opened.

"Good morning, Mrs. Fernhope. May I come in? I have a few more questions I'd like to ask you."

"Um, sure, Mr. Sovern."

She stepped aside, and he crossed the sill.

"A bit chill this morning," he said, "but very cozy in here."

"Stanley doesn't like the cold."

"Can't say I blame him."

Betty Sue took Sovern to the living room. "Have a seat."

He sat in a dark brown leather chair. Betty Sue sat on the sofa.

"Now, help me to remember," he began, "why Mrs. Fight thought it necessary to get a new pastor."

"She felt that Reverend Cole was behaving in a manner that was unfitting for her office. I mean, her behavior was without a doubt normal for a young woman. But as Mrs. Fight said, she was acting like a young woman, not a minister of God. She needs to get herself a husband."

Sovern scratched his head. "And what behavior might that be? What did Mrs. Fight think she was doing?"

"Well, you know how it is, Mr. Sovern. Young people these days. I mean, the Reverend is unmarried and she's with Mr. Thurgood."

"In what way is Reverend Cole *with* Mr. Thurgood?"

Betty Sue's face turned red. She coughed. "Well, um, Mrs. Fight has it on good authority that the Reverend Cole is having a sexual relationship with Mr. Thurgood. And that's not right. Her being a person of the cloth, you know."

"And who is this good authority?"
"She didn't say."
"Did you ask her?"
"Well, no, I didn't."
"Did anyone in your little club ask her?"
"No. No one did. You see, we didn't need to ask her."
"Why not?"
"Because everyone knows she's seeing Harry Thurgood. And, well, you know what men and women tend to do when they're alone with each other."
"Thurgood and the Reverend say they're just friends."
"Wouldn't you?"
"So you're saying Thurgood and Ms. Cole are having sex and because of that she needs to leave the church."
"Mrs. Fight thinks one's pastor should be above reproach."
"How do you know this good authority even exists?"
"Really, Mr. Sovern. Why would Mary Lou lie?"
"I don't know. You tell me."
"Mr. Sovern! Really. How can you say such a thing? Mrs. Fight is an upstanding member of our community."
Sovern pushed up his glasses and pinched the bridge of his nose. "Mrs. Fernhope, I can't move this case forward if I don't have solid evidence. You and your little club are telling me that there's substantial bad blood between Mary Lou Fight and the Reverend Ember Cole. That is a possible motive. But if I don't have any solid evidence..." He lifted his hands and shrugged.
"Reverend Cole a killer? Oh, my."
"There's no proof that she is. And with what you're telling me, which is just some sordid gossip, there's no motive either."
"Oh dear. But she could have run down Mrs. Fight to stop the..."
"Yes, she could. Which is why she's a person of interest."
"She is?"
Sovern nodded.
"So you think she might have tried to kill Mrs. Fight?"
"It's possible. She's a person of interest, but until I prove she was motivated enough to do so then that's what she'll remain. Just a person of interest. You're sure you don't know who Mrs. Fight's source is?"
Betty Sue shook her head.
"Okay." Sovern stood. "If you find out, you'll let me know?"

Betty Sue nodded.

Sovern wished her a good day and left.

In his car, he had a big grin on his face. "That will probably be all over town by sunset, and I'll be watching Thurgood's and Cole's reaction."

Chapter Twenty-two

SCARLETT HAYDEN WALKED INTO the Really Good a little before noon. Harry watched her unzip her jacket. At first he thought she didn't have anything on underneath, but, as she got closer, he realized she was wearing some kind of one-piece outfit. The legs were wide, giving the impression she was wearing a long skirt, and the neckline plunged to her navel, not that there was much fabric to form a neckline.

She sat at a table near the counter. Harry came out from behind the counter and crossed the floor to her table.

"Aren't you afraid you'll catch pneumonia?" he asked.

"Don't you like what you see?"

"I'm trying to be a gentleman."

She laughed a deep, throaty laugh. "Old-fashioned. Okay. I'll keep that in mind. Might be fun."

"Coffee? Lunch?"

"Actually, I have some information for you."

"Oh?"

"According to Betty Sue Fernhope, Reece Sovern was grilling her earlier this morning, and he told her he was pretty much set to arrest Ember."

"Why are you telling me? Did you tell Ember?"

"Oh, I figured you'd want to tell her." She reached out and touched Harry's arm. "I also want you to know that I'm here for you. In case you need someone to talk to."

"Thanks, Scarlett. Appreciate the gesture."

She stood and stepped close, a full on invasion of his personal space. Her perfume was subtle with a hint of musk. Deliciously seductive.

"It isn't a gesture, Harry. I'm your friend, and I'm here for you."

She touched his cheek, turned, and walked to the door.

He watched her leave. She didn't look back. *Damn, she's good,* he thought, then murmured, "The cougar must be getting tired of the youngsters." He shook his head and returned to his place behind the counter, just as Jessamine Walter, Charmaine Adler, Effie Snyder, and Opal Nussbaum walked in.

Wonder what Jessamine and Charmaine want with Effie and Opal? Are they recruiting new members already?

Harry smiled at the quartet and made his way over to their table. "What can I get you ladies? If you're looking for lunch, I have a bacon, potato, and leek chowder that will take the chill out of your bones."

Charmaine spoke, "I'll have my chamomile tea. You know how I like it." Harry nodded. She continued, "And that vegan sandwich."

"The tomato, tofu, kale, and sprouts on whole wheat?"

"Yes, that one."

"Got it. Anything for the rest of you?"

Effie ordered chili and cornbread with water to drink.

Harry smiled to himself at the order. *That's Ember's usual. Wonder if she's sending some kind of message?*

Jessamine ordered soup, a BLT on white bread, and iced tea. Opal got the same.

Harry walked back to the kitchen window and gave the orders to Miguel. He turned around, pretended he was wiping down his spotless counter, and cast a surreptitious eye towards the four.

Unlike, Mary Lou, Jessamine had them all in a seated huddle.

I wonder if Jessamine is making a power grab while Mary Lou is out of the fight? I wouldn't be surprised if she was. She's no different than Mary Lou, just cut from a finer cloth. If anything, she might even be more dangerous.

Miguel announced that the orders were up and Harry delivered them to the quartet's table. He wasn't able to catch anything of their conversation, as Jessamine made sure everyone's lips were zipped.

He puttered around the tables, not far from theirs, but to no avail. Their volume level would defy the navy's best SONAR.

Then four people walked through the door and he gave up his attempt at playing I Spy and focused on being a good store owner.

What he knew for sure was that he'd have to meet with Ember as soon as possible to let her know Sovern was gunning for her.

And if Neal was right, that meant the police investigator would be coming for him as well.

Chapter Twenty-three

EMBER READ HARRY'S TEXT. *Oh, my God*, she thought, *Reece is going to arrest me. This is it.* She put her face in her hands and stifled a sob.

Her phone dinged and she looked at the new text from Harry. *Be at the shop back door in five minutes.*

She took a deep breath and exhaled. "Ember Cole," she said out loud, "you've done nothing wrong. Even if you get arrested, there's no evidence against you. You've killed and hurt no one."

The thought, though, went through her mind: *This is all so doggone inconvenient and unfair.*

The time, according to her phone, was heading towards two-thirty. No wonder she was hungry. She'd been up and down Oak Street, as well as Adams. Some people had looked at her rather suspiciously, and now she knew why. A few of those she had visited were friendly. Most, though, were simply matter of fact.

She texted Harry back and told him she'd need ten minutes to get downtown from where she was. In a moment, she received a thumbs-up, switched on her moped, and headed for the parsonage. She'd drop off the moped and walk to the shop.

Ten minutes, however, turned out to be a bit optimistic. By the time she was pressing the buzzer for the Really Good's backdoor, she'd overstepped her estimate by two minutes.

Harry opened the door and let her in. He looked up and down the alley before closing the door.

"Were you followed?" he asked.

"I don't know. I wasn't paying attention. Why would, I assume you mean the police, why would they follow me?"

"To see where you go."

"If they are following me, they're going to have an awfully boring time of it."

"That's not the point."

"What is the point?"

"Sovern has a motive: you want to save your job and reputation."

"Murdering someone is going to do wonders for my reputation, and every church wants a killer pastor." She favored Harry with a grin.

"Ha, ha. Let's go upstairs and talk. I closed early."

"First, I killed Louisa. Then I run down Mary Lou. Now, I'm seeing you — alone — in your apartment. This is really doing wonders for my reputation."

"Probably being alone with me is worse than the first two."

"Bingo, buddy."

"Maybe I'll just have to make an honest woman of you, Em."

"Maybe, Angel Harry, you and I need to find the killer."

"Okay. Sounds like a plan. Upstairs so we can talk about it privately."

Ember followed Harry upstairs to his apartment. When she crossed the threshold, she took a look around. The room was large. A combination living room and dining area, which was conservatively and tastefully furnished. At least it looked tastefully furnished to Ember's eye. The furniture looked solid and not like the stuff you assembled out of a box.

"Nice place you have here."

"Thanks. Want a tour?"

"Some other time, perhaps."

"Something to drink?"

"Coffee?"

"Nothing stronger?"

"Isn't it a little early for that?"

"A hot gin toddy does wonders for the soul."

"Seriously?"

"Wouldn't lie to a woman of the cloth. Besides, I'm an angel. Remember?"

"Now you're making fun."

"Nope. You're set on a coffee?"

"Yes, please."

"Have a seat. I'll be back in a few."

Ember sat on the couch and looked at the painting hanging on the wall opposite her. It was a harvest scene, but it had an odd perspective. Exaggerated.

Harry returned with two cups of coffee. "Just like you like it, ma'am. Lots of cream and two sugars."

"Thanks, Harry."

"Did you find out anything of importance?"

"Not really," Ember said, and related the results of her visiting.

"Sad to say, I think you're right. Not much there. Not even Terresa was helpful." Harry then told Ember about his brief conversation with Scarlett.

"She likes you," Ember said.

"Not really. She's in lust. Probably tired of the kiddies." He drank coffee, then said, "I think you need to go away."

"Go away? I can't do that, Harry. I have a responsibility to my flock. Besides, wouldn't that make me look even more guilty?"

"Well, I—"

"No, I'm staying right here. I didn't do it. Which means Reece doesn't have anything on me."

"But he could make things very difficult for you."

"That's something I'll just have to deal with when it happens. In fact, I need to visit Mary Lou and pray for her."

"If you insist. But in the meantime, we need to ascertain who most likely wanted Mary Lou dead."

"Why not Louisa?"

"Just a guess, but I don't think Louisa Middlebrook was the real target."

"But if that's the case, why pick a Hat? That would be too suspicious, wouldn't it? Better a complete stranger."

"I suppose. If what you're saying is true, then whoever killed Louisa wanted her dead, and who on earth would want Louisa dead?"

"Someone who didn't like something she did. Or maybe didn't do."

Harry nodded. "So what did she do that so pissed off someone that they killed her for it?"

"I don't know. That's what just doesn't make any sense."

"But if you're right, and what you said makes perfect sense, then we need to focus on finding out everything we can about Louisa's life."

Ember nodded. "I can start by talking with Chris Hayes, her pastor."

"There's also Effie Snyder. You said she left Chris's church and joined yours to get away from Louisa."

"That's the talk."

"Why don't you start with Effie and Chris? I'll talk with Scarlett and see if she knows anything. Probably the other Hats, too."

"Scarlett?"

Harry shrugged. "She might have info, and if she's favorably disposed towards me, she might be willing to spill the beans."

"Uh-huh."

"What's that supposed to mean?"

"Nothing. Nothing at all."

"Right."

Ember stood. "I need to see Mary Lou. Not only will it look good, but she is one of my members and this is her time of need."

"Why don't I drive you?"

"If you don't mind?"

"Not at all. Want to go now?"

"Sure."

The two went downstairs, got into Harry's car, and drove over to the hospital.

"I'll go in with you, if you don't mind," Harry said.

"Sure."

They got out of the car and were halfway to the entrance when Reece Sovern spotted them and called out for them to stop. He trotted over to where they were standing.

"Excuse me," he said. "Ember Cole, I'm arresting you for the attempted murder of Mary Lou Fight. You have the right..."

Everything faded away for Ember. She heard the buzz of Sovern's voice and the angry questions shouted by Harry. She heard herself tell Harry to watch Wilbur for her. Then she found herself in a car, and the car was driving away from the hospital.

Chapter Twenty-four

HARRY WATCHED REECE SOVERN drive away with Ember Cole in the back of his car. When the car turned a corner and was no longer in view, out came his phone. He told it to call Lauderbach.

"Law office," the young female Texas accent said.

"Is Mr. Lauderbach in?"

"May I ask who's calling?"

"Harry Thurgood."

"One moment, please."

Classical music sounded in Harry's ear. Vivaldi, if he wasn't mistaken. Then he heard Stanton Mirabeau Lauderbach's baritone.

"Howdy, Harry. What can I do for you?"

"Sovern just arrested, Ember."

"Seriously?"

"Seriously."

"I'm on my way. You happen to know why?"

"No. Actually, he said he was arresting her for the attempted murder of Mary Lou Fight. If he said more than that, I didn't hear it, I was so angry."

"Don't worry. I'll find out."

"Thanks, Stanton."

"You're welcome."

The call ended, and Harry walked back to his car. He sat behind the wheel. This was not good. Having arrested Ember, Sovern would probably be looking at him next. And if the police investigator started looking, he'd be asking questions and digging up information. Questions Harry didn't want asked and information he definitely didn't want dug up.

Maybe he needed to disappear for a while. At least until the real perp was caught.

"Get real, Harry," he told himself. "Sovern has someone with a motive. He isn't going to look elsewhere unless he has to. His next step is to look at all of the people close to Ember to rule them in or rule them out."

He took a deep breath, slammed his hand on the steering wheel, and exhaled.

And of all the people in Magnolia Bluff, you, Harry Thurgood, are the closest to the Reverend Ember Cole.

He started the car. He needed to talk to Scarlett and the other Hats. He had to find a viable alternative to Em. Because if Sovern was no longer interested in her, he wouldn't have any interest in one Harry Thurgood, either.

However, even more important than getting Sovern off his back, he truly needed to get Ember off the hook, because without her in his life... Well, he just didn't want to go there.

***

A Ford Mustang was parked next to Scarlett's big Land Rover. He walked up to the door, and when it opened, out came a young guy as big as a refrigerator, and as black as midnight.

He looked Harry up and down, smiled, and said, "She sho do like to mix it up," and, chuckling, walked to the Mustang.

Harry watched the young man leave and found himself wondering how that moose of a guy could fit into that little car. He shrugged, turned back to the door, and pressed the doorbell.

He pressed it two more times before Scarlett opened the door. She was wearing a white robe, and had a towel wrapped around her hair.

"Harry Thurgood," she breathed.

"Hello, Scarlett. Have time to talk?"

"For you, yes." She pushed the door open. "Come in."

Harry crossed the sill. "Hope I'm not interrupting anything."

"You aren't. Can I get you something to drink? Martini?"

"Gin rickey."

"How do you make that?"

"Where's your bar? I'll do the mixing."

Scarlett smiled. "Now that's what I like. A man who can take charge. Four olives. I'm hungry."

She showed him the bar, and Harry went to work mixing the martini and the gin rickey. When the glasses were ready, he crossed to the couch where she was stretched out and handed her a glass.

"You've done that before, haven't you?"

He shrugged. "A good host knows how to take care of his guests."

"I like that. I like being taken care of." She sipped her drink. "Mm. You're good."

He smiled and took a drink from his own glass and sat in a chair across from her. "Sovern's arrested Ember."

"Sorry to hear that."

"Somehow I find that difficult to believe."

"No, I truly am. Ember's a nice woman. She's honest. No games. I like that." She drank a long swallow of gin with a whisper of vermouth.

"Somebody decided Louisa had to die. Who do you think that was?"

Scarlett shrugged. "Can't help you there, Harry. What I can tell you is that Mary Lou trusted her."

"Really?"

"Well, as much as Mary Lou trusted anyone. And Louisa would do anything for Mary Lou. I remember Louisa once said she was so grateful for being one of us, because she was no longer a nobody. People paid attention to her, once she put on the crimson hat."

He took a long pull from his glass and got more comfortable in the chair. "Would it be unreasonable to assume that even if Louisa and Mary Lou were attacked by the same person, that it might be for different reasons?"

Scarlett ate an olive, and a thoughtful look settled on her face. After a moment she gave a little shrug, ate another olive, and said, "Sure. That's possible. Why not?"

"And if Louisa and Mary Lou were attacked for different reasons, that means there might possibly be two killers out there instead of one."

"I suppose. But I don't see how that helps Ember. She could still be one of the two."

Harry's shoulders slumped. "Very true."

Scarlett ate another olive. "Have you talked to Neal?"

"Yes."

"If you ask me, even more than Mary Lou or that Terresa Brown, Neal has his finger on the pulse of this town. Go talk to him again."

He nodded. "I think you're right."

"Now that we got that out of the way, can I make a pizza for you?"

Harry noticed that Scarlett had let her robe start to fall open, and that she probably had nothing on underneath. "Uh, maybe another time."

He set his glass on the coffee table and stood. "Best try to catch Neal before he goes home."

Scarlett stood, but didn't bother to fix her robe. "Just remember, Harry, I'm here for you."

He smiled. "I haven't forgotten." He turned and walked to the door.

Chapter Twenty-five

JESSAMINE WALTER WAS NOT at all happy. She'd just gotten off the phone with Peyton Lindheimer, one of the nurses at the hospital, who'd told her Mary Lou had come out of her coma and had named Ember Cole as the driver of the car that hit her.

Jessamine told her phone to call Betty Sue, and when she answered asked if she'd heard the news.

"Yes," Betty Sue said. "My cousin, Gracie Fels, is a deputy at the jail, and she said Reece Sovern arrested Ember Cole about an hour ago. I guess Mary Lou was right all along. That woman is just a bad seed and has no place in our church. Or any church for that matter."

Jessamine sniffed. "I think Mary Lou is delirious. How could she possibly have seen Reverend Cole's face? Do you know how difficult it is to see anyone's face through a windshield?"

"Oh, I hadn't thought of that."

"I suppose not. I have another call coming in. Goodbye."

Jessamine put her phone down. This was not good. She needed to get Reverend Cole off the hook. She *had* to get her off the hook. All her plans for the future... What could she do? She went to the wet bar, made herself a Pimm's Winter Cup, and sat on the couch.

She did not want to think of that poor young woman sitting in a filthy dirty jail cell. Someplace where low life men had been kept. What would it take to get Reverend Cole out of jail, and at the same time make Mary Lou look like the ridiculous fool that she was?

Jessamine took a sip of her drink, and a big smile spread across her face. "Why, of course, give her an alibi." She took another sip of her drink. So what if she had to lie a little. She was positive that Ember would be so grateful to get out of jail, that, well, who knows just how grateful she might be. After all, it was her job, her livelihood, that was at stake here.

She took another sip of her drink. "Who knows how she might want to thank me?" A smile touched her lips, and soon spread across her face.

***

Ember's eyes took in the dingy yellow-green cinderblock walls for at least the tenth time. The interrogation room was bare except for the metal table, four metal folding chairs, and a light fixture in the ceiling. She noted that the table was bolted to the floor, and the folding chairs were chained to the table. Two cameras were situated in the upper corners of the room opposite her, as well as two in the corners behind her.

I guess the days of the one way mirror are long gone, she mused.

The door opened and in walked Reece Sovern. Another man was with him. Someone Ember had not met in the three years she'd been in Magnolia Bluff.

Sovern dismissed the police officer who'd been standing in the corner and took a seat opposite Ember. The other man remained standing, slightly behind Sovern and to his right.

The police investigator inclined his head towards the man. "This is Thomas Jager, our police chief."

Ember nodded. Jager said nothing.

"We're here, Reverend Cole, because Mary Lou Fight identified you as the person driving the vehicle that struck her. Our interview is being recorded—"

"There won't be an interview if my attorney isn't present. Fifth Amendment. Isn't that what it's called?"

"All we need is to get a few facts straight." Reece wasn't exactly pleading, but Ember thought he was getting pretty darn close.

She narrowed her eyes and looked directly into Reece Sovern's. "Read my lips. No lawyer. No talkie." She put thumb and forefinger together and drew them across her lips. Her arms folded across her chest, and her eyes went to the ceiling.

"Look, Reverend," Reece began.

"Forget it, Sovern," Jager said. "Terminating interview due to the accused's unwillingness to proceed."

The police chief stepped forward, put his hands on the table, and got inches away from Ember's face. She could smell his cologne and the taco sauce he probably had with his lunch.

"Playing hard to get isn't going to work, missy. We will break you. All your dirty, little—"

A knock on the door stopped Jager. All three looked at the dark gray metal rectangle, and then the door opened. In strutted Stanton Mirabeau Lauderbach. He had a black leather attaché in his hand.

"Well, gentlemen, Reverend," the lawyer began, "I see I got here just in time."

Jager spoke, "No, you didn't. We terminated the interview."

"Well, how about we begin again?"

"No, we aren't, Lauderbach," Jager replied.

"Very well, then, Mr. Jager. Now, if you don't mind, I'd like to confer with my client."

Sovern and Jager left, and the lawyer took a seat across from Ember.

"Did you say anything?"

"That I wanted my lawyer."

Lauderbach smiled that too genuine smile. "Very good. Probably royally pissed them off."

"The police chief for sure."

"They've arrested you based on Mary Lou Fight's verbal statement that she saw you driving the vehicle that hit her."

"Not possible."

"Remind me again why it's not?"

"I was at the parsonage, putting my home back together after the police search."

"And your cat will testify to that?"

Ember laughed, and then got serious. "I wish he could."

"That would be nice. Sovern still has your car, correct?"

"Yes."

"How have you been getting around?"

"My shoes and my moped."

"I'm going to see if Judge Jones will let you out on your own recognizance."

"He'd do that?"

"You have no priors, you are a minister with an obligation to conduct worship tomorrow, and you have no car at present, which means you are a low flight risk. I don't see why he shouldn't grant it." He looked at his watch. "We'll find out two hours from now."

"What happens in the meantime?"

"Unfortunately, you will be a guest of the wonderful warders we have here in Magnolia Bluff. There's nothing I can do about that. But I'm positive it will only be for two hours."

"And if it isn't?"

"Don't worry. You're my client. Even if we end up going to trial, I haven't lost a case in twenty years."

"I guess that's reassuring."

"It should be. And now, I have some work to do before we see the judge."

Lauderbach stood, and Ember slowly got to her feet. He went to the door, knocked twice, it opened, and a police officer entered.

"We're done here for now," Lauderbach told the man.

The lawyer left, and Ember followed her escort to the jail cell. She entered and sat on the bed. The door was locked, and she began to pray.

Chapter Twenty-six

HARRY GOT TO THE *Chronicle* just as Rebecca was leaving.

"Hi, Harry. I suppose you're looking for Neal."

"I am."

"He's not here. He's either at the courthouse or the police station. Sorry to hear about Ember."

"Thanks. It's a bummer. Say, do you know if he's been to see Mary Lou?"

"He tried, but the police aren't allowing anyone except family to see her."

"That figures. Courthouse or police station, you said?"

Rebecca nodded.

"Thanks. Have a good evening."

"You, too."

Since the courthouse was closer, Harry decided to stop there first. He trotted the couple hundred feet, climbed the steps, and entered the mammoth structure. Taking the steps two at a time, Harry arrived at the second floor, where the courtrooms were. There he found Lauderbach, but no Neal. The lawyer filled him in on the next steps. Ember was still in the holding cell at the police station. The deputies had not seen Neal, however.

Harry thanked him, and took off for the police station, which was located a couple blocks north of the courthouse. There he ran into Neal, who was just leaving the building.

"Waste of time, Harry. You won't be able to see Ember, and Sovern won't talk to you. Jager has everyone on a gag order."

"Is that normal?"

Neal shrugged. "Jager's kind of young for a police chief. Probably strutting his stuff, so to speak. I'm going to the courthouse. You know about the hearing to set bail?"

"I do. Ran into Ember's lawyer."

"Walk with me. We'll talk."

The two men left the police station for the courthouse. Harry filled his pipe. Neal began talking.

"The way I see it, Harry, Mary Lou's using this for maximum damage value. Even if innocent—"

"She is," Harry interjected, while lighting his pipe.

"Okay, so she is. But by the time this is over, too much water will have passed under the bridge. Her reputation will be shot, and she'll have to resign. At least that's how I'm guessing Mary Lou sees it."

"But that doesn't answer the question of why kill Louisa Middlebrook?"

"There is something there. Something brutal. Something personal. Which is missing from Mary Lou's hit and run."

"Two different people?"

"Possible. Probably not. The use of a car in both instances makes me think it was the same person who killed Louisa and tried to kill Mary Lou. In my experience, killers rarely change methods. They find what works for them and stick to it."

"But Reece hasn't found the vehicle yet, has he?"

"Not that he's saying. Lots of places a person can hide a vehicle, and if you have the right connections, you can run the car through a chop shop and make it disappear completely."

"People have those kinds of connections here?"

"People have those kinds of connections everywhere. You ought to know that."

"What's that supposed to mean?"

Neal let out a big laugh. "Don't go all indignant on me, Thurgood. It's as plain as butter and grape jam on white bread that you've been around. Just look at that hat of yours. There's not a goddamn person in Texas who wears a pork pie, except for some black jazz musician in Houston. And look at that suit. I doubt if Gunter Fight could afford one. No, my friend, there's no doubt you've been around. I just haven't figured out your game. Then, again, I don't need to. At least not yet."

"That's comforting to know."

"Enjoy it while you can and pray I don't have a slow news day."

"I'll do that. So does the use of the car mean the same motive's at work for Louisa and Mary Lou?"

"I think it means the same person is the perpetrator. As for motive, can't say yet. Which is probably why the Reverend Cole was only charged for the hit and run."

They arrived at the courthouse. And Neal asked if Harry was going in.

"No. There's something I need to check on."

"Okay. See you around."

Harry walked back to the *Chronicle* and retrieved his car. It was time he talked to Ember's closest friend. The closest other than himself.

Chapter Twenty-seven

JESSAMINE PARKED HER JAGUAR in front of the city hall and walked around back to the police station. The officer on desk duty asked how he could help her.

"I have some information for Reece Sovern pertaining to Ember Cole."

"He's not here at the moment. Can I give him a message?"

"It's very important that he get this. Can I call him myself?"

"He'll be in court very soon."

"Oh, dear. What's his number?"

The officer looked up Sovern's number and gave it to her.

"Is this his cellphone?"

"No, it's his desk phone. Here at the station."

"I need to talk to him, *now*. What's his cellphone number?"

"I can't give that out, ma'am."

"Oh, good God. An innocent young woman's life is at stake here."

"Sorry, ma'am. Procedure. You can call and leave a message, or I can give him a message."

"Is Tommy Jager in?"

"No, he's not here. He's either at the courthouse or he's gone home for the evening."

Jessamine marched back out of the station to her car. She drove the two blocks to the courthouse, parked, got out, and entered the building.

"Now where?" she muttered. The courthouse was a big place and Sovern could be anywhere. *But if he was due in court...*

She took the elevator to the second floor. When the doors opened, she exited, and began checking courtrooms.

There were five in all. The first two she tried were locked. The third revealed Wylie Garrison haranguing some poor soul about something. She closed the door and moved on to the fourth.

There she could make out that Judge Jones was holding forth about something. She opened the door and peered in. There was the county attorney, Richard Hildalgo. Behind him were Tommy Jager and Reece Sovern. On the other side of the courtroom were Ember and her attorney.

Jones was saying, "I've looked over the evidence submitted by Mr. Hildalgo on behalf of the city of Magnolia Bluff. I've also considered the request for bail to be set at two hundred and fifty thousand dollars, and the argument from Mr. Lauderbach that the amount is excessive, given that Reverend Cole has been a minister in good standing in her denomination, has been an upstanding citizen of Magnolia Bluff, is not a flight risk, and should be free to discharge her duties to her flock. Mr. Lauderbach also makes a very valid point concerning the fitness of Mary Lou Fight to make a statement at this time.

"Therefore, I'm releasing Reverend Cole, on her own recognizance. Ms. Cole?"

Ember stood. "Yes, Your Honor?"

"What that means is that when you are summoned by this court, or your presence is requested by any law enforcement official, or by the county attorney, you are to appear post haste. Do you understand?"

"Yes, Your Honor."

"Good. And Mr. Sovern?"

"Yes, Your Honor?"

"Are you done with the Reverend's car?"

"We are, sir."

"Then get it back to her today. She needs it for her work."

"Yes, sir."

"This court is in recess," Jones said, and banged his gavel.

Well, that was a stroke of good luck, Jessamine said to herself. *Now to put the icing on Reece's day.*

Chapter Twenty-eight

HARRY PULLED UP OUTSIDE Effie Snyder's house and put his car in park. He took in a deep breath, exhaled, shut off the engine, and climbed out.

Her home was made of stone and was rather small in the German-style of many early Hill Country homes. Harry guessed it might be one of the original houses in Magnolia Bluff.

He walked up the porch steps and rang the doorbell. The door opened a crack. He took the initiative. "It's me, Effie. Harry Thurgood. I'd like to talk to you about Ember."

The door opened all the way, and Harry was face to face with the almost tiny woman. Her eyes were red. Evidently, she'd been crying. At least that was Harry's guess.

"I heard they arrested her. Is it true?" Her voice trembled and was barely above a whisper.

"It is. May I come in?"

"Okay."

She opened the door, and Harry walked into the house. The entryway was small. She closed the door and indicated he should follow her into a room that was to the left. He did so, and found himself in a small living room. There was a fireplace on the far end, and a fire was burning in the grate. On the mantle were groups of small figurines.

The hardwood floor was covered with a large area rug. Pole lamps were situated in the corners.

There was a sofa and two chairs, with a coffee table between them. A large vase, on the table, contained a dried flower arrangement. Between the chairs was a small table with a lamp on it.

Effie sat on the end of the sofa by the fire and indicated a chair. "Have a seat," she said.

Harry sat. Above the couch was a plain, dark brown wood cross. On the coffee table, next to the vase, was a large Bible.

Looking at her, Harry couldn't help but think he'd seen someone else that looked like her, but for the life of him he couldn't think who it was.

"You wanted to talk about Reverend Cole?" she asked.

"I'm trying to find information that will guide the police to the real killer."

"I see. I don't know how I can be of help."

"You're probably her best friend—"

"I don't know about that, Mr. Thurgood. She's very fond of you."

"She is?"

"Yes, she is."

"Well, then, I guess we are two very lucky people. Aren't we?"

Effie smiled. "I guess we are."

"Now, we both know Ember wasn't involved in the murder of Louisa Middlebrook and the hit and run of Mary Lou Fight."

"Mary Lou is a terrible person. She's pure evil. She calls herself a Christian, but she's a wolf in sheep's clothing. She's the Devil, going about seeking whom she may devour."

"You won't get much of an argument from me on that score. Now, you were also Louisa Middlebrook's friend. Do you know of anyone who might want to see her dead?"

"I *was* her friend. But Mary Lou ruined her. Turned her into a Becky Sharp."

"Pardon me?"

"Thackeray. *Vanity Fair*. In the book. The social climber. Becky Sharp used people. And that's what Louisa Middlebrook became: a user."

"So are you saying there are lots of people who wanted to see her dead?"

"Oh, yes, Mr. Thurgood. She became a very bad woman. Faithless."

Harry raised his eyebrows. He couldn't help it. The intensity in her voice, and the look in her eyes made him think, for a moment, she'd lost it. This was one very obviously hurt woman. He cleared his throat, and Effie lost the crazy look.

"Well, if lots of people wanted to see her dead, that isn't much help. Is it?"

"I guess not."

"Which means it will be difficult to get Ember off the hook. We need a more likely suspect to hand over to Reece Sovern."

"There's Charlese Erikson. She and Louisa were best friends since grade school. She became depressed and had to be hospitalized. Stopped going to church altogether."

"Anyone else?"

"Talk to her friends. They're all suspects."

Harry pursed his lips, nodded, then asked, "Why does Mary Lou have it in for Ember? Any reason in particular? Or is it just because she's mean and nasty?"

"I've heard it said around church that Mary Lou was very fond of the former pastor. Maybe too fond. . . if you understand what I mean."

"I think I do. So Reverend Cole is more or less an innocent victim here."

Effie nodded. "She's a good person. She cares about people. Cares about me."

"That's what I like about her, too. And she's fun to be with."

Harry noticed Effie had a faraway look on her face, as though he wasn't even there. When she spoke, her voice was soft, as if she was talking to herself. "She's the shepherd looking for the sheep that's lost and when she finds her she'll hold her and comfort her and save her from the storm."

"Well, I've taken up enough of your time." He stood. "I best be going."

Effie looked up at Harry's face. "She's fond of you. But she's the Lord's Anointed. The pleasures of this world are not for her. You remember that."

"Certainly, Effie. Certainly. I'll remember."

Harry took his leave and pointed his car in the direction of the Methodist parsonage. On the way, he voiced his thoughts out loud, "That is one odd woman. I wonder what her background is? And more importantly, is she an actress in this drama of ours?"

Chapter Twenty-nine

REECE SOVERN READ AGAIN the statement he'd taken from Jessamine Walter. He'd said nothing when she'd given it, but he knew something fishy was going on. According to Jessamine, she'd stopped by the parsonage to talk with Ember Cole and was doing so at the same time someone was running down Mary Lou Fight.

He picked up his notebook and turned to the page where he'd jotted notes from his conversation with the Reverend. She'd made no mention of having any visitors and had even made that quip about not knowing she'd be needing an alibi.

The investigator set the notebook down, picked up the statement from the Walter woman, and read it once more.

"One of them is lying, and a dime to a doughnut it's Jessamine Walter. But why?" The coat rack had no answer for him. But he continued talking to it anyway. "What horse does *she* have in this race?"

He pondered the information while getting a cigar out of his drawer. He removed the cellophane and stuck the stogie in his mouth.

"I bet it has something to do with that damn society. Bunch of rich women with too much time on their hands. God."

He put his hands behind his head and his feet up on a corner of his desk. With eyes closed, cigar jutting out of his mouth, he began mentally sifting through the information he had gathered, trying to find the kernels of wheat, the kernels of truth, amongst all the chaff.

The murder of Louisa Middlebrook was intentional and brutal. The ME's report identified two blows to the back of Louisa's head. Both made with a cylindrical object, probably a baseball bat. They had rendered Louisa unconscious and may have eventually caused her death. But that wasn't enough for the murderer. He, or maybe she, had laid the victim on her back on a hard surface, probably asphalt, given the particulate matter found on her clothes and skin, and driven a vehicle over the body twice. Once would've been enough because the first tire had crushed Louisa's chest. The second pass had crushed her skull.

To Reece, the violence of the death indicated the murder was personal. Someone, friend or relative, had been royally pissed off to the point that they planned and carried out the Middlebrook woman's death.

Following that line of thinking, Sovern concluded that the possibility of two murderers existed. Unless he could establish a strong connection between Louisa and Mary Lou, and the only connection he saw there was that women's club of Mary Lou's.

"Which brings us to Jessamine Walter," he murmured. "Perhaps this all boils down to a battle for control of that group of busybodies. But murder?"

Sovern couldn't bring himself to go down that road. No, the person who killed Louisa was someone she knew and who she had royally ticked off. That was the only premise that made sense. Now he just had to find out who that person was.

As for Mary Lou, she'd ticked off plenty of people in town. There were undoubtedly dozens of people with motive. Lots of motive. For her, it only made sense that one of those people had said enough was enough and had tried to do her in. The death of the Middlebrook woman probably spurring them on.

Mary Lou, though, was alive and Louisa Middlebrook wasn't. He'd focus his attention on Louisa. He'd heard she'd snubbed people when she took up with Mary Lou's group. He wondered how many she'd snubbed, and how many resented the snubbing? Resented it enough to finally decide it was time to get even?

Chapter Thirty

HARRY WATCHED EMBER PARK her car in front of the parsonage. He got out of his BMW and met her as she got out of her compact.

"News travels fast in this town," she said.

"Don't you know it."

"How did you know I was released?"

"I'm an angel, remember? We angels know these things."

"I suppose you do. Lauderbach told you, didn't he?"

"Actually, we angels are not limited by space and time."

She laughed. "Yeah, right. Maybe you should write science fiction during the slow periods at the coffee shop."

"Maybe I should at that."

"So why are you here?"

"To see you."

"Okay, you see me. Now what?"

"May I buy you dinner?"

"I don't know, Harry. I'm emotionally exhausted. A raincheck?"

"How about I cook for you?"

"Boy, that will really get people talking."

"Probably not any more than they already are. Tell you what."

"What?"

"Take a long hot shower while I rustle us up some grub. You'll feel better. Plus, I do have some questions I need to ask you."

"Seriously?"

"Yes, seriously."

"Being an angel, don't you just know things?"

"I do. But not what's inside your head."

She laughed. "That's a copout if I ever heard one. Okay. Rustle up some grub, and I'll take a shower."

"Have a preference?"

"Corned beef hash, if you can find it."
"I'll be back!"

***

Harry opened a bottle of Texas Syrah and poured wine into two glasses. He handed one to Em, opened the bag, and took out their dinners.

"Corned beef hash, as only the Silver Spoon can make it, along with a garden salad and French dressing. And for *moi*, meatloaf, mashed potatoes and gravy, and a side of corn."

"Smells heavenly," Ember said, while bending close to the container.

"Dig in."

She took a forkful of hash and conveyed it to her mouth, moaning with pleasure.

"With everything that's been going on, do you have a sermon ready for tomorrow?" He swallowed wine, and then put a bite of meatloaf in his mouth.

She put her fork down. "I don't know if anyone will bother to show up. Even if they find the killer, I'm finished here. I might even be finished with the ministry. What church would want me?"

"Oh, ye, of little faith. My guess is that tomorrow you'll need overflow seating. Everyone will show up to hear what you have to say. It will be your chance to shine. So I'd say make sure your message is a good one."

"Come to think of it, you're probably right. Curiosity killed the cat, but satisfaction brought it back."

"Very true, that old saw. Probably half the town will be at your church seeking satisfaction. The other half will be saying, I can't get no—"

Ember held her hand up. "That isn't some song reference, is it?"

Harry shrugged. "Might be."

Ember rolled her eyes.

"In any event, it will be your time to shine, my friend."

She reached out and touched his arm. "Thank you for being my friend, Harry. I can't tell you how much your support means to me."

"I'm glad I can be here for you, Em. You're my best friend."

"Oh, go on." She picked up her fork and filled it with hash.

"No, I mean it. You are the best friend I have."

"I'm glad."

Harry could see she was very tired, so he didn't press the conversation. They finished eating mostly in silence.

With food and wine gone, he collected the containers and put them back in the bag, along with the empty wine bottle, and stood.

"I'll see you in church tomorrow."

"You will?"

"Yep. I'm your angel, remember? I'll be watching over you."

She stood and put her arms around him. Harry caught a giant whiff of perfume. "I love you, Harry Thurgood." Her voice was soft, barely audible.

"I love you, too, Em."

She pulled back, and Harry looked into her eyes.

"But not that kind of love, Harry. We're friends. Best friends."

"Okay, Em. Best friends."

He kissed her cheek. "Goodnight. Get some sleep, and I'll see you tomorrow."

They walked to the door, where he touched her arm, said goodnight again, and left.

When he was behind the wheel, he looked over to the house and saw her standing in the doorway. He started the car, returned her wave, and drove back to his place.

"I didn't get to ask my questions. Oh, well, I guess they can wait until tomorrow."

His mind shifted to his talk with Effie Snyder, and that made him shudder.

Chapter Thirty-one

HARRY FIXED HIMSELF A Corpse Reviver No. 1. For a winter evening tipple nothing beat the mix of cognac, Calvados, and sweet vermouth.

He sat in his easy chair, sipped his drink, and put in a call to Neal Holland.

"Shouldn't you be sleeping?" the gruff voice asked.

"Probably. I didn't wake you, did I?"

"I'm a newspaper man. I never sleep. Might miss a story. So what can I do for you, Harry?"

"What do you know about Effie Snyder?"

"Born and raised here in Magnolia Bluff. Went to school here and the college. Always lived here except for a couple years right after college. Don't know where she went. That's a page out of her book she doesn't talk about. Devout Baptist. Practically hard shell. So it was something of a surprise when she showed up at the Methodist Church. That gave the gossips something to talk about for a couple months."

"Must've been some fight between her and Louisa Middlebrook."

"Not that I'm aware of. Although, according to those who know, Louisa did snub her after she joined Mary Lou's group. Apparently, she snubbed all her old friends. Put them right off."

"But Louisa was a newcomer, wasn't she?"

"Yep. Been here close to ten years. What's all this interest in Effie?"

Harry told Neal about his visit.

"Sounds like Effie. She always could put the hell in hellfire."

"That bad, eh?"

"She's serious with a capital S about her faith."

"She never married?"

"Never did. Don't think she ever had a boyfriend. At least none I heard about. You think there's something there?"

"Possibly. She's taken to Ember, that much is obvious. She also detests Mary Lou."

"So you're thinking if she likes the Reverend and learns that Mary Lou is trying to get rid of her, that might be enough to drive Effie to do something?"

"That's what I'm thinking."

"Sounds good to me. I'll see if I can find anything to help you build a fire."

"Thanks, Neal. Have a good evening."

Phone call ended, Harry picked up his pipe and tobacco pouch, filled the old briar that had been his grandfather's, and lit the fragrant mixture.

He sipped his drink and puffed on the pipe. He asked himself: *if Effie got angry enough, would she try to kill someone? Would she try to run down Mary Lou? And if she ran down Mary Lou, had she already killed Louisa? Could that crazy, devout little woman, in fact, be a coldblooded killer?*

Chapter Thirty-two

REECE SOVERN WAS NOT a religious man. Facts were his stock in trade, not belief systems. Facts lead to the truth. Beliefs were opinions about the truth and were often a far cry from the truth.

Yet there he was sitting amongst the faithful at the First Baptist Church of Magnolia Bluff, listening to Reverend Chris Hayes delivering the morning message. Hayes was apparently preaching through the book of Romans. His text for that morning was Romans 2:1: "Wherefore you are without excuse, O man, whosoever you are that judges: for wherein you judge another, you condemn yourself; for you that judge others practice the same things."

How appropriate, Sovern thought. *Maybe Hayes should get one of those vans with a loudspeaker on the roof and broadcast his sermon to the town.*

When the service was over, he made his way to the pew where Ron Middlebrook was sitting. He waited until those offering condolences had left and then sat next to the man.

"Hello, Ron."

"Hi, Reece. You haven't been here for a long time."

"True enough."

The big man nodded.

"I'd like to ask you about Louisa's friends."

"You'd be better off askin' one of those crimson hat women."

"I'd like to know who her friends were when she came to Magnolia Bluff."

"Back when we got married?"

"That's right."

"Geez, I don't know if I can remember."

"Think back. She was new in town. Who did she meet first? Were her friends all here, at church? Can you remember any of her friends from where she lived before?"

"In Austin?"

Sovern nodded.

"I don't know, Reece. I mean..." Ron Middlebrook buried his face in his hands.

"This is hard, I know. But I need to know who Louisa knew. And the sooner I get the information, the sooner I can find who killed her. You want me to do that, Ron, don't you?"

The big man lifted his head and swiped at his eyes with the backs of his hands. "I do. I want you to get that son of a bitch."

Sovern put his hand on Ron's shoulder. "Good. Stop by my office this afternoon and we'll compile a list. How's that?"

Middlebrook nodded. "I'll see you after I get something to eat."

Sovern stood and waited while Reverend Hayes finished greeting the last of his congregation. When everyone had left, he approached the minister, who was standing near the door with his wife.

"Good to see you, Reece."

Sovern shook hands with the minister. "Very appropriate message." He gave a nod and a smile to Mrs. Hayes.

"All things work together for the good, you know."

"If you say so."

"Paul, actually."

Sovern smiled.

"I assume you're here on business."

"I am. Can we go somewhere and talk? Perhaps your office?"

"Sure." Hayes turned to his wife. "I'll just be a moment."

She smiled in response.

Sovern followed Hayes to the minister's office, where he motioned for Sovern to take a seat. Hayes sat across from him.

"What's on your mind, Reece?"

"I'm trying to get a list of Louisa Middlebrook's friends."

"Not sure I can help you with that. You'd be better off talking with Rhoda. Let me text her."

Sovern nodded, and Hayes tapped on his phone. A moment later, Rhoda Hayes joined them, and Chris explained what the police investigator was looking for.

She thought a moment, and then said, "I remember when she first started coming here, she was sort of shy. Didn't have a lot of self-confidence. She tended to be self-deprecating. Always talking about how overweight she was. I was probably her closest friend, until she met Effie. Then those two were like Siamese twins. They did everything together. Which we thought odd at first because Louisa was nowhere near as conservative as Effie."

"Louisa, though, back then, was more pliable," Chris put it.

"Yes, she was. Maybe that is what made that relationship work. Once she got involved with Mary Lou Fight, she began to change. But to answer your question, Mr. Sovern, Louisa was friendly with everyone, but closest to Effie and then me. As far as her friends here at church. I wouldn't know about any other friends she had.

Sovern stood, thanked the Reverend and Mrs. Hayes for the information and took his leave.

On the drive back to the station, he admitted he might have made a mistake. The Reverend Ember Cole just might not be the guilty party. Then again, she might be the puppet master pulling the strings. On the other hand...

"I need to talk to Effie Snyder. She just might be in this right up to her eyeballs, with or without the Reverend Cole directing the choir."

Chapter Thirty-three

EMBER, SEATED OFF TO the side of the pulpit, had never seen her church this full. The pews were packed. Folding chairs lined the back. The doors were open to the narthex, where people stood jammed together. The proverbial sardines in a can.

The organ stopped playing, Ember stood, stepped up to the pulpit, and raised her hands.

A tomato hit her shoulder, and was followed by the word, "Murderer!"

"You need to leave," someone shouted.

Ember lowered her hands. Her eyes took in the faces staring at her. Some were angry, more were curious, and most looked on in curiosity wondering what she would do next. How she'd handle the situation.

She raised her hands again, and said, "This is the day which the Lord hath made: let us rejoice and be glad in it."

She ducked and the egg hurled at her splatted behind her.

From the back of the sanctuary, came a lyric baritone singing:

Amazing grace! (how sweet the sound)

That saved a wretch like me!

I once was lost, but now am found,

Was blind, but now I see.

Ember smiled. Her angel to the rescue. She, Effie, and a few others joined in as Harry began the second stanza.

By the end of the second stanza, the organ was playing and at least half the people were singing. That's when Gunter Fight stood and marched out of the church, followed by dozens of others.

When the hymn was over, Ember noticed about half the people had left. She looked at those who remained. Most were her people, some were curiosity seekers from town, but they were all people and they needed to hear about God's love.

She said, "Once, I was lost. I was a wretch. God's love was not visible to me because I was blind. But the grace of God, through our Lord Jesus Christ, brought me home.

"And such are we all. But our God is gracious. He's a loving God. He is our portion and our shield, as long as life endures.

"I want to say, I love all of you. And I loved Louisa Middlebrook. She was nothing but kind to me. And I love Mary Lou Fight, who I see as a sister in the faith.

"There are some, in this church, who think I'm not fit to be a minister. Perhaps they are right. But I have not intentionally done anything to harm anyone.

"Job was a righteous man. That was God's argument against Satan's accusation that Job only worshipped God because God protected him.

"But Job did make a mistake. In countering the arguments of his three friends, he justified himself rather than God. I shall not make that mistake. God is always just. He sent his Son to show us His mercy. I have done nothing wrong, but I am in the hands of my Lord and Savior. And if I have done something wrong, I trust He will show me and lead me to repentance.

"Whatever happens, I will praise His name. I hope you will, too. Amen."

Again that lyric baritone filled the sanctuary.

Rock of Ages, cleft for me,
Let me hide myself in Thee;
Let the water and the blood,
From thy riven side which flowed,
Be of sin the double cure,
Cleanse me from its guild and power.

And again the congregation joined in. When the hymn was over, Ember raised her hands, said the benediction, and told everyone to go forth in peace.

When the last person was gone, she stepped down from the pulpit, and walked to the last pew where Harry Thurgood was sitting.

"I didn't think you were religious," she said.

"I'm not."

"So where did you learn those hymns?"

"I'm an angel, remember?"

"How can you be an angel and not be religious?"

"God's ways are not our ways."

"But you aren't God, mister."

"No, I'm not. I'm just an angel doing his bidding."

"Well, thank you, Harry Thurgood, my angel. Thank you for getting me out of a jam."

"My pleasure. Want to get something to eat?"

"What part of 'I don't think this is a good idea' don't you get? I'm in scalding hot water. My reputation has been shredded."

"Does that mean you can't have lunch with a friend?"

"You are impossible, Harry Thurgood."

"No, I'm your friend. Now get out of those robes, and let's get something to eat. You've told them you're innocent. Now show them."

Chapter Thirty-four

SOVERN'S CONVERSATION WITH RON Middlebrook wasn't overly productive. Even though Louisa was the love of his life, he knew little about her life prior to them meeting online.

Louisa Middlebrook's parents were dead. She had two siblings she wasn't close to: a younger sister who lived in New York City, and an older brother who was in the navy, currently stationed in Japan. She kept in touch with a former college roommate, who lived in Dallas, but aside from her name, Ron knew nothing about her.

After they were married, and Louisa moved to Magnolia Bluff, she was friends with Rhoda Hayes and Effie Snyder and was friendly with the other women in the church. But after she joined Mary Lou's Crimson Hat Society, "those women had all her attention and nobody else mattered," according to Ron.

"What I'm lacking," Sovern said out loud, "is motive. Why did someone want Louisa and Mary Lou dead?"

He looked over his notes. "Most crimes take place because of money, and that includes murder, but I'll be damned if I can see how someone would gain financially from their deaths.

After money, comes revenge, elimination of a rival, and jealousy." Sovern sighed. "With those three, I can probably find half the town guilty. Although that probably holds true more for Mary Lou than Louisa. But if I do eliminate gain, then the motive is most likely one of those three. Which means someone saw those women as rivals to be eliminated, or had been wronged by them and wanted revenge, or was jealous of what they had and decided to do something about it."

Sovern got to his feet. By all accounts, Effie Snyder had taken Louisa's snubbing very badly. "Time she and I had a chat. Let's see if revenge fits her."

***

Mary Lou was not a happy camper. Not that she'd ever gone camping in all of her sixty-some years. Gunter had just told her how that no good Harry Thurgood had saved the day for Reverend Ember Cole with his theatrics.

Gunter had replied with, "Don't worry about it, my dear. The police are working on it, and if they don't make progress soon I'll see to it that the Rangers are brought in."

Of course, Gunter completely missed the point. Mary Lou wanted to see the person suffer. To beg and plead for her leniency, her mercy, and then see the look of doom on their face when she said no.

Being in the hospital was counterproductive to her plans. She wanted to go home. But a shattered hip and a badly broken leg meant she wasn't going to be walking the dog anytime soon. Not that she had ever walked the dog in her life. However, being laid up in the hospital meant her plans to get rid of Ember Cole would most likely have to be put on hold, for this year at least, what with the multiple surgeries and many, many months of therapy that were in her future.

She needed to meet with her girls, but that Sovern wouldn't hear of it. So the society business would have to wait. Unless she could have a phone conference with them, or one of those video conferences that were all the rage. Yes, that was the answer. Maybe she'd have a new pastor yet come July.

***

Jessamine Walter had invited the members of the Crimson Hat Society and their husbands for dinner after church.

When the meal was over, the men retired to the den with their coffee and pecan pie, while the women moved to the living room.

"I'm taking this time to discuss some important society business," Jessamine said.

"Can we do that?" Betty Sue asked. "Mary Lou is the Queen. I don't think we can conduct business without her. Can we?"

"Of course we can," Charmaine answered. "Four of the five members are present, and Jessamine is the acting chair."

"Don't we have to vote on that?" Betty Sue asked.

Charmaine sniffed her annoyance. "Very well if you insist. Who doesn't want Jessamine to chair our meeting?"

Scarlett drank coffee and Betty Sue fidgeted.

Charmaine continued, "Go ahead, Jessamine."

Jessamine took a sip of coffee before speaking. "I heard from my friend, Arlesue, that Mary Lou will need several surgeries and extensive, long-term therapy before she'll be able to walk again. And that's being exceedingly positive."

"How does your friend know this?" Scarlett asked.

"Her husband golfs with Dr Rayburn. He's the one who is doing the initial surgery. This very afternoon."

Scarlett nodded and ate pie.

Jessamine continued, "To make sure our society continues to operate, I propose that you agree to appoint me Queen until Mary Lou can once again attend our meetings. Any objection?"

"Can we do that?" Betty Sue asked. "Shouldn't we check with Mary Lou?"

"Mary Lou's time is going to be spent in surgery, recovery, and therapy," Charmaine said, and added, "For a very long time."

"Yes, but—" Betty Sue, didn't get to finish as Charmaine cut her off.

"We need a Queen who can direct our activities. Mary Lou may *think* she can do it, but you heard Jessamine. We need an active leader. I'm in support of Jessamine being Acting Queen of the Crimson Hat Society until Mary Lou Fight is fully recovered and can take over the duties incumbent with the office of Crimson Hat Queen. Is anyone opposed?"

Scarlett ate pie, and Betty Sue fidgeted.

Jessamine smiled. "Good. Now that we have that settled, I want to propose a new member to replace our dear, departed sister Louisa Middlebrook. I propose the Reverend Ember Cole."

A Mona Lisa smile touched Scarlett's lips. *Let the fireworks begin.*

Chapter Thirty-five

POLICE INVESTIGATOR REECE SOVERN rang Effie Snyder's doorbell. There was no car parked at the curb, save for his own, and he couldn't recall if Effie even drove a car. He'd have to take a walk up the alley and check the garage.

He was about to push the button a second time when the door opened, and he was face to face with the small, intensely serious woman. She asked how she might help him. Sovern replied by telling her who he was.

"I know who you are," she said. "What do you want?"

"I'd like to ask you a few questions."

"What about?"

"The death of Louisa Middlebrook and the hit and run involving Mary Lou Fight."

"Go ahead and ask."

"May I come in?"

"No."

Sovern raised his eyebrows but said nothing. This was simply Effie being the contrarian that she so often was. At least according to the word about town.

"Perhaps this isn't a good time?" he said.

"It won't ever be a good time. What do you want to ask?"

"Well, let's get this out of the way first."

Effie cut him off. "I was at home when Louisa was killed. I have no one to corroborate that. Didn't know I'd be needing someone to tell you I was in bed and asleep. And I was in the backyard weeding my vegetables when someone tried to kill Mary Lou Fight. I'm not sure if one of the neighbors saw me or not, and the Brussel sprouts aren't talking."

A smile crept up on Sovern's face as he made a note in his notebook. "How would you describe your relationship with Louisa and Mary Lou?"

"It has nothing to do with me. She attacked the shepherd. I am defending the shepherd. I'm helping the shepherd of God's flock to keep the wolves at bay."

"I see. And what you just said was in reference to Mrs. Fight?"

Effie nodded.

"What about Louisa? I heard tell you two were pretty close at one time."

"We were. But she fell under the spell of the one going about seeking whom he may devour."

"You mean Mary Lou?"

"Yes. She corrupted a Godly woman and turned her to the ways of the world."

"Sounds to me like maybe that's something Mary Lou would need to answer for."

"You said it, Mr. Sovern, and she will. In this world or the next."

"Sometimes God uses a human agent, though, doesn't He?"

Sovern observed Effie, watching for any kind of reaction. All she did was look at him, her face blank, then said, "Sometimes He does. But that's for Him to decide, isn't it, Mr. Sovern?"

"I guess it is at that."

"I have things to do, so I'm going to bid you a good day." And with that, she closed the door. Sovern heard the deadbolt slide into place.

He walked back to his car and got in. "That is one strange woman." He pushed his lips out and closed his eyes, held that position for a moment or two, and then got a cigar out of his suit coat pocket and removed the cellophane. He ran the stogie under his nose and then stuck it in his mouth.

"Just as cotton was king, there's something going on with Effie Snyder. What, though, is the question?"

Chapter Thirty-six

Jessamine Walter parked her car in the student parking lot at the college. She got out and walked down to the river. The spot was not clearly visible from either the river or the school grounds. A quiet little glade nestled amongst the cottonwoods lining the shore. She broke through the trees, and he was there. Waiting.

"Yo, Mrs. Walter, you're late."

"Keep your voice down."

"No one can hear us, 'cept the squirrels, and they ain't gonna tell nobody nuthin'."

She dug in her purse and pulled out an envelope. "Here. Are you ready?"

"I'm ready. When?"

"Whenever. But make it sooner, rather than later. Just don't get caught."

"I won't get caught. You can be sure o' that."

"Good." Jessamine turned to walk away. When she felt his hand grasp her arm, she stopped. "What is it?"

"Ain't you forgettin' the other part of our deal?"

"Are you serious? I have to get back."

"A deal's a deal, Mrs. Walter."

"Fine. Just hurry up."

***

Harry dropped Ember off at the parsonage and drove back to his place.

They'd talked about Effie while at lunch, but Harry quickly discovered Ember didn't know much of anything about the little woman's past. He ran over their conversation in his mind.

"Do you know anything about a person named Charlese Erikson?" he'd asked and added, "Effie seemed to imply she might have something against Louisa."

"Never heard of her. Does she live in town?"

"Don't know. I've never heard of her either."

"Sorry, can't help you."

"Effie also said Louisa was a user, like Becky Sharp in *Vanity Fair*."

"Is that a book?"

"Yes. By Thackeray."

"Never read it."

"Don't bother. Most of it is a snoozer. Anyway, Effie implied Louisa made lots of enemies. Chief among them this Charlese Erikson."

Ember shook her head. "I don't think so. It seems to me that Effie's projecting."

"Maybe. If it is, she took the loss of Louisa's friendship harder than anyone's thought."

"That's probably true."

The topic quickly ran out of steam after that, so they'd discussed other things.

Harry entered his apartment, made himself a pink gin, fired up his pipe, and called Neal.

After pleasantries were exchanged, Harry said, "Effie mentioned a Charlese Erikson as being a friend of Louisa's since grade school, and that she became so depressed after Louisa broke off the friendship that she was hospitalized. Effie implied this Charlese might be a suspect."

"Not possible."

"No? Why not?"

"Louisa came here from Austin ten years ago. Charlese Erikson committed suicide before Louisa ever arrived here."

"Then why would Effie tell me such a cock and bull story?"

"You're new. Probably figured you'll chase down that story and leave her alone."

"How long does a person have to live here to not be new?"

"In your case, even your great-grandkids will be newcomers. Hell, if your ancestors didn't live here in the days of the

Republic, you're a newcomer in the eyes of many. Welcome to life in a small town."

"Wow. Okay."

"I remember a few years ago a family moved here from Dallas. Wanted to get away from the big city. They bought a few acres and were going to go all green and do sustainable farming, or some such. Anyway, I recall the wife complaining one day to someone at the Silver Spoon that every time she called someone on the phone, no matter what the nature of the call was, she always got the third degree. All manner of questions about her. And she was getting really sick and tired of it. Her friend told her that no one knew who she was, and because everybody is either related to or knows everyone else, the people had to establish who she knew so they'd know what was safe to tell her."

"You're kidding."

"God's truth. I'd swear to it on a stack of Bibles."

"Huh. Guess I'll always be a newbie. I'll remember that. But getting back to Effie, why tell such an obvious lie? She had to know I'd find out sooner or later."

"That, I can't tell you. But what is interesting is that Charlese Erikson was friends with Effie Snyder and killed herself after Effie left town."

Chapter Thirty-seven

SCARLETT HAYDEN STEPPED INTO Harry Thurgood's apartment. He closed the door while her eyes took in the room.

"Cozy," she said, and added, with a smirk, "I like your air freshener."

"Are you talking about my pipe tobacco?"

"I am. Nothing makes a man look more distinguished than a pipe."

Harry merely smiled, then asked, "May I get you a drink? Or, if you care to tag along, I was going to get supper at Olivia's."

She moved close enough so she could touch his arm and let him catch the scent of her perfume. "Or we could have it delivered."

"That's true. Although, I was looking forward to rubbing shoulders with the hoi polloi."

"Aren't my shoulders good enough for you? They're very nice shoulders, you know."

"Oh, I'm sure they are."

Scarlett moved away and sat in a chair. "May I ask a personal question?"

"You can ask."

"Are you into boys by chance?"

Harry raised his eyebrows and said, "No. What makes you think I might be?"

"Ember. She looks like a boy. She's as flat and curveless as they come. Don't get me wrong. I think she's a sweet person, but I think her libido registers in negative numbers."

"Perhaps you don't know her as well as I do."

Scarlett stood and crossed the room to stand face to face with Harry. "I can tell you this, Mr. Thurgood. All you have to say is giddy up, and I will give you the ride of your life. Anytime you want."

Harry took a step back. "Thanks for the offer, Scarlett. You said you had some information you thought I might like to know?"

She returned to the chair. "I'll take that drink now. Martini. Four olives, please. I'm hungry."

Harry made her drink and fixed a gin rickey for himself. He handed the glass to her and took a seat in a chair opposite. He raised his glass, and said, "Skoal."

Scarlett raised hers. "Here's mud in your eye." She took a large swallow.

Harry sipped his drink and she watched him looking at her, waiting. Should she try to force the issue. Or should she just drink her drink, tell him her news, and leave.

"Okay, Harry, you win. You're in love with Ember and that trumps every asset I have. But if and when you fall out of love, will you look me up? I'd love to love you."

"Deal."

She took another large swallow of her drink and ate two olives. "Here's the news. Jessamine Walter has performed a *coup d'etat* and taken over the Crimson Hat Society. Her first order of business was to propose Ember Cole for membership. Charmaine was all in favor. Betty Sue was probably opposed but didn't say anything. And I, quite honestly, don't care. So probably tomorrow Jessamine will be talking to Ember about becoming a member of our pathetic little group."

"Do you know Jessamine's reasoning?"

"Stick it to Mary Lou. Kick her while she's down. Jessamine's from Charleston. She's from an old antebellum family. Why she's probably the closest thing to us having a duchess as we'll ever get. She can't stand Mary Lou, and I think she's been planning this for a long time. Besides, she hates living here in this backwater. She's a true Southern Belle, and we're Hicksville. I think she wants to gentrify us."

"Interesting." He thought a moment, then said, "Four olives probably won't curb your appetite. Join me for pizza?"

Scarlett downed the remainder of the martini, ate the olives, and stood. "Harry, hon, what will satisfy this appetite is you. And you don't seem to be on the menu. I think I'll just mosey on back home and make do with the second string."

Harry stood. “I’m flattered, Scarlett. I really am. Just wish we were on a different timeline.”

“Story of my life.” She walked up to him, kissed his lips, and said, “See ya around, lover.”

She opened the door and left. Once in her car, she let out a big sigh, and drove home. All the way back, she wondered what Jessamine’s purpose was in asking Ember to join the society. There had to be more to it than just sticking it to Mary Lou.

Chapter Thirty-eight

HARRY FINISHED HIS DRINK, decided he still wanted pizza, and walked over to Olivia's.

When he entered the restaurant, Olivia gave him a wave, and said, "A good evening to you, Mr. Coffee Man."

Harry chuckled, and said, "Glad I'm not Mr. Olson."

Olivia gave him a puzzled look, and since there was no one over thirty in the place, save for himself, he smiled, said, "Old TV commercial," and took a seat.

In a moment, Olivia was at his table. "Was there a Mrs. Olson?"

"There was. Check YouTube. I'll have pepperoni and mushroom on thin crust."

"No fish? Hot date?"

"Nope. It's not Friday."

She gave him a funny look, then asked what he wanted to drink.

Harry thought a moment. "Your house red is pretty good. I'll have a glass of that."

Olivia left to place his order. Harry got out his phone and called Ember's number.

"Hello, Harry."

"I'm at Olivia's. Join me? Only college kids here."

"Honestly. Twice in one day?"

"The coffee shop is closed, and I always see you twice when it's open. I'm just keeping the routine going. Besides, Scarlett thinks you're skinny and that you need a few curves."

"Oh, she does, does she?"

Harry nodded his thanks to Olivia for the wine. When she left, he continued, "She does. Not that I agree with her."

"You're seeing an awful lot of Scarlett these days."

"Not enough, according to her."

"Maybe you should take her up on her offer."

"Can't. Being your guardian angel is a full-time job."

"I see."

"What kind of pizza do you want?"

"I didn't say yes."

"You didn't?"

"No, I didn't."

"Huh. Thought you did. Olivia's got your pizza in the oven, so I hope I got it right."

"Seriously?"

"Would I lie to you?"

"As a matter of fact—"

"Don't say it. I'll see you in ten."

"You are incorrigible. I think I should ask for a posting in Taiwan."

"Why? Just make my job harder."

"All right, *friend*, I'll see you in a few."

Harry smiled at the phone. *God, I* am *in love with her*. He picked up the wine glass and took a sip. *But how to break through that shell? That's the question*.

He still hadn't come up with an answer, when a slim, jean and sweater-clad figure slid into the booth opposite him.

"Okay. I'm here. Where's my pizza?"

At that moment, Olivia brought Harry's pizza to the table.

He said, "You got that Canadian Bacon and black olive pizza cooking, don't you?"

Olivia didn't miss a beat. "Yep. It's on. And what will you have to drink, Ember?"

"Root Beer."

"Coming right up." Olivia cast a smirk in Harry's direction and headed on back to the kitchen.

"No anchovies?"

"It's not Friday."

"Ha, ha. Don't go into comedy."

Harry grinned at her and assured her he wouldn't think of it. Ember took a slice of his pizza.

"Why do you like spending time with me? I'm not going to put out."

"Geez, Em, that's pretty blunt. But I already told you. Did you forget?"

"Harry, we can't go there. And because we can't, won't you get tired of me?"

"No." He picked up a slice of pizza. "Besides, if that's what I wanted, Scarlett's literally throwing herself at me. And speaking of Scarlett, she told me that Jessamine ousted Mary Lou as Queen Bee of the Hats."

"No. Seriously?"

"That's what she said."

"I can't believe it."

"And there's more. You're going to get a visit from Jessamine and she's going to invite you to join the Hats."

Ember's eyes grew big and round, and then she started laughing.

"What's so funny?"

"Me? A Hat? Oh, my God, that's the funniest thing I've heard in months. Why?"

"Why you for the Hats?"

Ember nodded. Her mouth full of pizza.

"Scarlett didn't know."

She swallowed pizza. "Well, I'll be... Probably just to stick it to Mary Lou. You know: 'Ha, ha. You're in the hospital and can't stop me.' I bet that's what it is."

"Probably. So, are you going to don the Crimson Hat?"

"Heck no."

"Didn't think so."

Olivia was back with Ember's pizza, and both she and Harry took a slice. Before taking a bite, Ember said, "I did get a strange call from Effie."

"How strange?"

"She was going on and on that I needn't worry. That she was going to protect the Lord's Anointed. By which, she meant me."

"That is strange. Do you think she's lost it? Gone off her rocker?"

"I don't know. Maybe."

"Perhaps we ought to call adult protection." Harry ate pizza and sipped wine.

"I don't think we should go there. At least not yet."

"Okay."

"I'm going to get a box for this. I'm tired. Been a stressful few days."

"That it has. How'd you get here?"

"I walked. It's not that far."

"Mind if I walk you home?"

"Would it do any good if I said I did?"

"What? Can't hear you."

"Thought so. Okay. Although it is completely out of your way."

"It's a small town."

Ember laughed. "That it is."

Harry signaled the waitress, as he didn't see Olivia, and asked for boxes and the check. He put enough bills on the table to more than cover the cost and the tip, and when the pizzas were safely boxed, the two left the restaurant.

"Here," Harry began as he shifted to Ember's right, "a gentleman always walks on the street side when he's with a woman."

"Is that so? And why is that?"

"I suppose to protect you from the mud and filth of the street."

"How very seventeenth century of you."

Harry heard the squeal of tires and the high revving of an engine. He turned and saw headlights bearing down on them. He shoved Ember away from the street and leaped after her seconds before the car sped by. Harry felt the tailwind roll over him.

"Are you okay?" he asked Ember.

"I have a rip in my jeans and skinned heels on my hands, otherwise I think I'm okay. This pizza, though, is done for."

"Let's get my car, it's closer, and go to the ER."

"I don't think that's necessary. And there's nothing they can do for the pizza."

"Don't *you* go into comedy." Harry winced. "I might have twisted my ankle. Hurts like the devil."

"Okay. ER it is. Can you walk?"

Harry tried to stand with Ember's help and shook his head.

Ember got out her phone. "I'll call Reece. He'll be more than glad to help."

"No. Call Neal. We'll tell Reece later."

Ember told her phone to call the newspaperman.

Harry leaned back against the building, and said to himself, *This just got personal. Very personal.*

Chapter Thirty-nine

HARRY UNLOCKED THE COFFEE shop door. The only person waiting to get in was Fergus.

As usual, the old drunk's morning comments were somewhat off the wall.

"Good morning, Mr. Thurgood. Still too cold for May. But that's what comes of bad blood. Deceive your friends and it'll bite you in the ass and make for a cold May. Mark my words."

Harry said he'd think about it.

"Mark my words," Fergus called out as he took a seat at a corner table.

Harry hobbled over to his table in the corner of the coffee shop and sat.

Behind the counter was Jack Bonhoffer. He had a smile on his face, and Harry knew he'd done the old retiree a good deed.

Cleaning and prepping the tables was Miguel's cousin, Estrelita. Another good deed. She could use the money for college.

"If I had to get a sprained ankle, at least it came at a good time," he murmured.

He drank coffee and took a bite out of one of the four doughnuts on his plate. The door opened and in walked Reece Sovern. He marched over to Harry's table and took a seat.

He took the cigar out of his mouth. "And you were going to tell me about this attempted hit and run when?"

"Man, news does travel fast in this little burg."

"Well?"

"In about five minutes. But you beat me to it."

"Yeah. Right." He shoved the cigar back into the corner of his mouth.

Harry lifted his hands and shrugged, then said, "Coffee?"

"Sure. Why the hell not? With everything else turning to a stinking pile of manure, might as well drink a cup of coffee while I'm looking for a shovel."

Harry got Estrelita's attention, held up his coffee cup, and pointed to Sovern. She smiled, nodded, and headed for the coffee pot.

"Want breakfast?" Harry asked.

"Had oatmeal. Thanks anyway."

Estrelita placed the cup of steaming black liquid in front of the detective and left.

Sovern took a sip, murmured, "Ah," set the cup down, and said, "Did you get a license plate number? See the driver? Better yet, can you tell me who did it?"

"Strike three. You're out."

"Thought so." Sovern drank coffee. "Who do you think was the target? You? The Reverend? Both of you?" He drank more coffee.

"Don't know."

"What the hell do you know, Thurgood? Because I know you're working with Holland to get a big scoop for his paper." Sovern leaned across the table. "And I don't like a couple of amateurs making a mess of my investigation. Savvy?"

Thurgood held up his hands. "Look, Sovern, getting your shorts in a bunch, and turning cooperative folk into uncooperative isn't going to help you."

"I could toss you, the Reverend, and Holland into the clink as material witnesses. What do you say to that?"

"I'd say you're not stupid, and that would be a very stupid thing to do. We'd be better off working together."

"Oh, we would, would we?"

Harry nodded.

The door opened and in walked Ember. Before she could reverse direction, Sovern saw her, and waved her over to the table.

Harry watched the stoic mask descend on her face. He smiled inwardly. Em had strength. Resilience. She'd weathered all of Mary Lou's machinations just fine. And that made him love her all the more.

"Good morning, Mr. Sovern," she said, while holding out her hand. He took it and they shook hands. She sat in the chair he indicated.

"Thurgood's telling me we should all work together to solve this case. What say you?"

"Sounds like a splendid idea."

"Splendid, eh?"

"Yes."

Estrelita stopped at the table and asked if anyone would like to order.

"I'd like my usual," Ember said, then chuckled. "You probably don't know what that is."

"I do. Mr. Thurgood told me."

"He did, did he?"

"Yes. I'll get it right away."

"Anything for you, Mr. Sovern?"

"More coffee, please."

Estrelita left and was back in a flash with coffee for the Reverend and the police investigator. "Your breakfast will be here in a minute, Ms. Cole." And she left again.

"You going to keep her, Harry?" Ember asked, then sipped coffee.

"I think so. Probably hang onto Jack, too."

"You going somewhere?" Sovern asked.

"No. But having them here will give me more flexibility. I won't be tied down like a farmer with dairy cows."

Sovern nodded and turned to Ember. "Did you see anything last night?"

"Just the headlights. Harry shoved me out of the way. The car was gone by the time I got back on my feet."

"And no idea if they were after you, Thurgood, or both of you?"

"Sorry. No."

Sovern inhaled enough air to create a vacuum in Lakewood Church, then exhaled. "Well, it looks pretty obvious that one or both of you were the target."

Estrelita set Ember's fried egg sandwich on wheat toast before her, asked if anyone needed anything, and when everyone said no, she left.

"For what it's worth," Harry said, "I think Ember's the focal point."

"How so?" Sovern asked, then drank coffee.

"It seems to me, Mary Lou's decision to oust Ember from the church is the starting point. My guess is she ordered the Hats to collect all the dirt they could, and in doing so triggered someone to try to stop her."

"But murder? And why Louisa Middlebrook?" Harry could see Sovern was skeptical.

"From what I've heard, Louisa was devoted to Mary Lou. I think someone killed Louisa to send a message to Mary Lou. When the message went unheeded, the killer went after Mary Lou."

Sovern thought a moment, then said, "If you're right, then that makes you the target last night. Why?"

"I don't know. But to reinforce that this is about stopping Mary Lou, Jessamine Walter's taken over the Hats and wants to make Ember a member."

Sovern looked at Ember. "You know about this?"

"From Harry. He told me last night."

The police investigator leaned back in his chair and closed his eyes for a moment before sitting up and saying, "I think things might be starting to make sense. I just don't see why someone would want to run you down, Thurgood. How do you fit into this?"

Harry shook his head. "I have no idea," he said out loud. *Last night might have nothing to do with your case, Detective. It might be the past trying to get even with the present.* And the palms of Harry's hands were suddenly very moist.

Chapter Forty

BETTY SUE FERNHOPE WAS shaking, visibly shaking. Mary Lou Fight was on the other end of the phone reading her the riot act.

"I had to find out from JoLinda Tremaine that my girls, *my* girls, turned against me in my hour of need. Why didn't you stop this, Betty Sue? Why?"

"I tried," Betty Sue whined, "but no one listened to me."

"It's too bad Louisa wasn't there. She would have derailed the whole thing. And now I can't do a damn thing about it. I'm trussed up like a turkey for Thanksgiving. And that Jessamine won't return my calls or answer my texts. You have to fix this, Betty Sue."

"But how? Jessamine and Charmaine had everything all organized. And, and Scarlett just sat there. What can I do?"

"Let me think. I'll come up with something, and if you grow a backbone, I should be able to force them out."

"They want Ember Cole to be the new member."

Mary Lou's scream of rage was so loud, Betty Sue had to hold the phone at arm's length. When the decibel level had dropped, she brought the phone to her ear in time to hear Mary Lou yelling at someone that she didn't want to be sedated and then the phone went silent.

Betty Sue looked at her phone. The call had ended. She put her phone down, walked into the kitchen, and made herself a hot chocolate.

She sat at the table and stared out the window, sipping her drink. After a time, her voice just above a whisper, she said, "I wonder if Jessamine will let me go back to my old church?"

***

Scarlett drank coffee and thought about Darryl's slip of the tongue during their sex play. He called her "Jessamine" just before his orgasm. She didn't say anything or question him then or after. But the more she thought about it, the more she wondered just who the Jessamine was that her boy toy was referring to. Someone back home? Or someone at the college? Or someone here in town?

The only Jessamine she knew of in town was Jessamine Walter. And that put a smile on Scarlett's lips. Did that pretentious hoity-toit occasionally like a little dark meat?

"Wouldn't that make a nice bargaining chip?" she said out loud.

She drank coffee and continued her musing. "In fact, if Mary Lou found out, Jessamine Walter would probably never dare show her face in town again."

Another swallow of coffee. "Hell, maybe I could become Queen of the society." She smiled. "If I did, I think I'd disband it. That would be a real kick in those old biddies' knickers."

She laughed at the audacity of the idea. Laughed long and hard. When the laughter died down to the occasional chuckle, she drank coffee.

"Ought to be easy enough to find out. Those muddle-headed jocks all bragging in the locker room... I'll just start asking my boys. I'll know who this Jessamine is soon enough, and if it's our new Queen?" She giggled. "Oh, that will be so delicious."

***

Jessamine Walter walked into the Methodist church office. Sitting at the reception desk was Effie Snyder.

"How may I help you, Mrs. Walter?"

"Is Reverend Cole in?"

"She is. Have a seat. I'll let her know you're here."

Jessamine sat on one of the wooden chairs, while Effie poked her head into one of the offices. After a moment, Effie returned, motioned for Jessamine to follow her, and ushered her into Ember's office. Ember was standing in front of her desk.

They exchanged good mornings, shook hands, and Jessamine sat in the chair indicated by Ember's outstretched arm. Ember sat across from her.

Jessamine took in the young woman, dressed in black, sitting before her. She looked so sweet, so wholesome. And she was the prettiest young thing Jessamine had seen since leaving Charleston. All she needed to do was to get her out of that uniform. Get her to start wearing some colorful dresses. She licked her lips, and then her musing was interrupted by Ember's voice.

"How may I help you, Mrs. Walter?"

"I am inviting you to join the Crimson Hat Society of Magnolia Bluff. I think you'd make a wonderful addition to our group. While we are a society devoted to the mutual support of women and to having fun, I think you would bring a certain gravitas. To help us keep our fun wholesome and pleasing to the Lord."

"I'm surprised and honored, Mrs. Walter. I truly am, but I cannot accept."

"And why not? Being a member of our group will certainly raise your standing in our community. And that can do nothing but help you bring the word of God to our fair city."

"I don't doubt that for a minute. But if I accepted all of the memberships offered to me, I wouldn't have any time to do the work of this church. Don't get me wrong. I'm honored, very much so, but I will have to decline."

"I am so very sorry to hear you say that." Jessamine paused a moment. There had to be some way to get Ember to join. Then it came to her. "How about this, Ember, I hope you don't mind me calling you by your given name."

"It is my name."

"And such a lovely name it is. Makes me think of a warm fire on a chilly winter's night."

Ember smiled.

Jessamine smiled back and continued, "Perhaps you could be an honorary member. That way you wouldn't be actively involved but would still reap all the benefits."

"I don't know, Mrs. Walter..."

"Please, Ember, call me Jess. All my friends do, and I hope we can be friends. Good friends. And given recent events, I think you might find a friend helpful."

Jessamine Walter stood, and Ember did also. She took a step forward and touched Ember's arm and let her fingers trail a bit down her sleeve. "I hope to see you wearing a crimson hat soon. A good day to you, Ember."

"And may the Lord be with you, Mrs, er, Jess."

Jessamine left the office and the church and got into her car. Having Ember in the society would be wonderful. But being her friend would be infinitely better.

Chapter Forty-one

HARRY'S PHONE RANG. HE answered and said, "Hey, Em."

"Jessamine just left."

"Did you get your hat?"

"She offered and I declined. Then she wanted to make me an honorary member, but I think the whole thing was just a come on."

"What do you mean?"

"Just that. I think she was coming on to me."

"Are you sure? Does this happen often?"

"Look, Harry, when I—"

There was just silence. Harry checked his phone to see if there was still a connection. "Em? You there?"

"I'm here. Must've been a momentary hiccup. I'm not that pure and innocent to not know a come on when I hear one."

"Okay. If you say so. Even so, what if she did?"

"What if Jessamine is the one behind all this?"

"And her motive is because she likes you?"

"Not like, Harry, but *like*."

"You mean as in Sappho?"

"Give the guy a cup of coffee."

"Huh. That would be a curve ball no one saw coming."

"Something to think about."

"That it is."

"I have to run. Just wanted to let you know that your good buddy Scarlett was right."

"She's not my good buddy."

"Yeah, right. Ciao."

Harry looked at his phone. Call ended. He shook his head and thought about what Ember had said.

"I wonder if Neal knows? Maybe we should chat. Just might wrinkle his newsprint."

***

Reece Sovern rang the doorbell at the Walter residence, and when no one answered the door, pounded on it. After a minute, he gave up and walked back to his car.

"I suppose Mister is at the college giving a lecture. But where the heck is Mrs. Walter? Would she be up this early to talk to the Reverend? I suppose she just might at that. Get a new member and solidify control of that gossip group."

He took a cigar out of his pocket and studied it for the longest time. Finally he took off the cellophane wrapper and put the stogie in his mouth. He worked it over to the left corner and held it there.

Sovern thought of the alibi Jessamine Walter had provided for the Reverend. It was obviously fake. Then she ups and dethrones Mary Lou Fight and takes over the group. And follows that up with recruiting the Reverend Cole, who Mary Lou was trying to fire.

"Looks to me like Jessamine is all in for the Reverend. The question is why? And is there a murder motive hiding somewhere in all of that?"

He shook his head. He just couldn't see a murder coming out of that group's political maneuverings. Just couldn't.

Jessamine's car pulled up in front of the house. He watched her get out of the car, go up the walk, and enter through the front door. Reece followed and rang the doorbell.

When the door opened, he said, "Good morning, Mrs. Walter. May I come in? I have a couple questions I'd like to ask you."

She hesitated but a moment, before saying, "Not at all," and stepped aside so the investigator could enter.

Sovern walked in, looked around, and then followed Jessamine to the living room. He sat in a chair and she on the sofa facing him.

"How can I help you?" she asked, while looking at her watch.

Sovern got the message and decided he'd ignore it for as long as possible. Make her sweat a bit. "I want to know why you fabricated that alibi for the Reverend Cole."

"I'm sure I don't know what you mean."

"Of course you do. Reverend Cole's statement contradicts yours. And I'm sure the Reverend would have been aware of your presence had you been there. So let's cut the crap. Why did you lie for the Reverend? Did she ask you to?"

"No, she didn't. I was just trying to help. She's being railroaded by Mary Lou Fight, and I... Well, I just wanted to help."

"I could write you up for interfering with an investigation."

"Oh, dear. I didn't realize..."

"I'm not going to," he said, paused, then continued with, "if you help me out."

"Sure. Anything."

"Why does Mrs. Fight have it in for Reverend Cole?"

"I'm not Methodist, but from what Mary Lou has said, I think it's because Ember doesn't cater to her. The former pastor, well, truth be told, liked women. I don't think he ever did anything inappropriate, but he liked their attention. And he gave them attention to get it. And Mary Lou ate that up."

"If I'm understanding you, you're saying Reverend Cole doesn't play favorites."

"No. At least that's what I've heard."

Sovern took the cigar out of his mouth and, not seeing an ashtray, stuck it in a pocket. He pushed his glasses up and said, "Do you think that Mrs. Fight's campaign to get a new pastor might be the motive for Mrs. Middlebrook's death and the attempt on Mrs. Fight's life?"

"That would be rather extreme, wouldn't it?"

Sovern shrugged. "People will kill each other over five bucks or burnt lasagna."

"I suppose there are people like that. Not my people, though."

"And who are your people, if I may ask?"

"The Middletons and the Chestnuts. The leading lights of Charleston. I'm surprised you need to ask."

"This is Texas, Mrs. Walter. We're a long way from South Carolina."

"Yes, we are. A very long way."

To Sovern, it seemed her voice was filled with an ocean of regret.

He said, "To clarify, you don't think Mrs. Fight's campaign to oust Reverend Cole had anything to do with the murder of Mrs. Middlebrook, or the attempted murder of Mrs. Fight."

"I really couldn't say. What is obvious is that Ember can no longer be hurt by that harridan. Or perhaps harpy would be a better term."

"Are you aware that someone tried to run down Harry Thurgood and Reverend Cole last night?"

Sovern watched the color drain from Jessamine Walter's face.

"N-no. I, I wasn't aware of that."

"Any ideas why either or both would be targeted?"

"No. None." After a moment's pause, she added, "If you don't mind, Mr. Sovern, I'm not feeling well."

"Sorry to bother you. A good day to you, Mrs. Walter, Hope you feel better."

Reece Sovern left, and as he got into his car he couldn't help but think it odd that both Effie Snyder and Jessamine Walter seemed to be emotionally involved in some way with the Reverend Ember Cole.

Chapter Forty-two

WITH THE HELP OF his cane, Harry hobbled across the square to the *Chronicle* office. When he opened the door and walked in, Rebecca Wilson asked, "What the heck happened to you?"

Harry told her about the near miss the previous night.

"Lucky you. And Reverend Cole. I don't think Neal would want to write your obits."

"He would if it sold papers."

Rebecca laughed. "You're right there."

"Is he busy?"

"He's always busy. But he'll make time for you. Hobble on over."

Harry hobbled over to Neal's desk and sat in a chair. The newspaper publisher turned from his computer screen, and asked, "Who'd want to run you down?"

"That's what Reece wanted to know. I have no idea."

"I see. We're assuming it's you they wanted and not the Reverend. Right?"

"That's my guess."

"So what do you, Louisa Middlebrook, and Mary Lou Fight have in common?"

"That's a good question."

"Which is why I asked it. It's the question we need to answer to get to the bottom of this."

"You think so?"

"I know so."

"Okay. While you're pondering that, what can you tell me about Jessamine Walter?"

"Not much. Prominent family and money back in Charleston. Husband got a teaching position at the college about a dozen years ago. He's had several books published. Jessamine's a prominent member of the garden club. Been in Mary Lou's group for around ten years. Plays bridge on Thursdays. Drinks Pimms pretty much exclusively although she does indulge in the occasional mint julep."

"What about her sex life?"

"Don't know. Rumor has it that Dr. Walter has more than a casual interest in pretty, young coeds. But he's never been caught *in flagrante delicto*, nor has any coed ever complained about him."

"Nothing on Mrs. Walter?"

"No. Why? You have something?"

"Ember thinks Jessamine was coming on to her this morning when she was extending the invitation to her to join the Hats."

Neal whistled. "Seriously?"

"That's what Ember said. But I can't imagine—"

"A woman making a pass at the Reverend? You do know this is the twenty-first century, Thurgood, don't you?"

"Yes, I do, Neal. It's just that Ember's pretty doggone chilly when it comes to sex."

"I think you need new glasses, Mister. And it might not be sex per se. Might be the authority figure."

"What do you mean?"

"Some women are drawn to authority figures. And ministers are authority figures. As for you, she might be extra frosty because she likes you."

"You think?"

"Yeah, you need glasses. So the Reverend thinks Jessamine was coming on to her. Well, I'll be..." He chuckled. "The local bloviators and babble-merchants would love to get hold of that little tale."

"The *blo* what?"

"Bloviators. A neat little word President Harding popularized for gossips."

"Hm. Learn something new every day. But you know nothing about Jessamine's sex life?"

"'Fraid not. This little tidbit is the first I've heard. Might be worth finding out if there's any scuttlebutt back in Charleston."

"Perhaps. Not sure what bearing it would have."

"Harry, we're trying to put together a puzzle for which we have no picture. We don't know what information will provide the picture so we can put all the pieces together. Jessamine liking young women, if she does, may or may not have a bearing on this case. But we won't know until we can establish it as fact and add it to all the other facts."

"Okay. Makes sense."

"Good. As I see it, Ember Cole is the epicenter of this little earthquake. Everything flows back to her."

Harry stood. "Thanks, Neal. Have a good day."

"I will, if Murphy stays away."

Harry hobbled across the room, said goodbye to Rebecca, and slowly made his way back across the green to the coffee shop.

On the way, he asked himself what he, Louisa, Mary Lou, Jessamine, and Effie all had in common with Ember. And for the life of him he couldn't come up with anything other than, "We all love her or hate her."

Chapter Forty-three

EMBER HAD ALMOST LET it out talking with Harry. She'd have to be extra careful. No one could know. No one could ever know. It would be the end of everything if anyone found out.

"Be sure your sin will find you out," she murmured, and shook her head. "That's all in the past and it's staying there." She bowed her head and whispered, "I believe You've forgiven me, Lord. Please help me to forgive myself."

She got up, left her office, told Effie she was going out for a walk, and left the church.

With her voice a barely audible whisper, she said, "Jessamine takes over the Hats when Mary Lou is out of commission. She then offers me a chance to join the Hats. Me, who is Mary Lou's nemesis. What if Jessamine orchestrated all of this just so she could get me in the Hats, where I'd be close to her. Then at some point make an advance towards me. If only Harry knew. He thinks I'm naive and innocent." She laughed, and the laugh was bitter. "I'm far from naive and innocent, Harry Thurgood. Wish to God I was."

She swiped the backs of her hands across her eyes, took a deep breath, exhaled, and continued musing. "So if Jessamine wants some kind of relationship with me, and went to all the trouble to take over the Hats, did she also kill Louisa and try to kill Mary Lou in order to set her plan in motion?"

Ember shook her head. "I suppose it's possible, but it sure as heck doesn't seem probable."

By Texas standards, this was a chill January day. Temperature in the low fifties. She shivered and wished she'd put on a heavier jacket.

"But if Jessamine did kill Louisa and tried to kill Mary Lou, did she also try to kill Harry? Anybody with eyes can see Harry likes me. Is Jessamine also trying to get rid of the competition? Possible, I suppose. But that car was heading for both of us. What if I was the target?"

She shivered and turned around to go back to the church. "If I was the target, then why was Mary Lou run down? Unless Mary Lou was trying to draw attention away from herself. But does she hate me enough to want me dead? God help her if she does."

***

Reece Sovern sat in his car and looked at the reservoir while eating a doughnut and drinking coffee. Close to noon and the park was pretty quiet.

The chill morning must be keeping everyone at home, he thought.

He drank coffee and took a bite of his doughnut. His mind sifted through the data he'd collected on the case.

Louisa Middlebrook rendered unconscious and then driven over by a car or truck. Body dumped in the cemetery. By all accounts, Mary Lou Fight's staunchest supporter.

Mary Lou Fight. At least half the town hates her guts and fears she knows their deepest and darkest secrets. She starts a campaign to oust Ember Cole as pastor of the Methodist Church, then she becomes a victim of a hit and run.

Was Louisa's death a signal to Mary Lou? And if so, why Louisa? Why not one of the other Hats? Being her right-hand woman, did the killer think her death would have the most impact?

The attempt to run down Harry Thurgood, or the Reverend, or both. Probably the attempt was against Thurgood. But why? Is it because he likes Ember Cole? That would reinforce a jealousy motive. But jealousy on whose part?

"What's in the killer's mind regarding Thurgood that I'm not seeing?" Sovern asked himself.

He took a bite of doughnut, drank coffee, and continued to stare at the reservoir. The thoughts swirling in his head.

Effie Snyder is very protective of Cole, and Jessamine Walter wants her to be a member of what's now her group. Why? What's in it for Jessamine to have Ember in the Crimson Hats? There has to be more to this than that damn gossip group.

And Effie. Now there's a nut job if there ever was one. Kill two birds with one stone perhaps? Get rid of the one person who turned against her *and* was now going to go after the person Effie's devotion was focused on. Then, after getting rid of Louisa, kill Mary Lou, who's the source of all the problems?

"If I put Reverend Cole in the center," he said, "then Louisa and Mary Lou line up against her. On the other side, there's Thurgood and Effie for the Reverend.

"Jessamine, who's in Mary Lou's camp, switches sides and supports Cole."

He pushed his glasses up and scratched his head. "Thurgood's for the Reverend, yet he is almost run down. How the hell does he fit in?"

Sovern pursed his lips. "Could Jessamine or Effie, or both, see Thurgood as competition for Ember's attention? If so, this case just became a whole lot more personal. And if it's personal, were either or both, Jessamine and Effie, eliminating a romantic rival? Or simply moved by jealousy?"

The police investigator smiled. "Affairs of the heart. Those cause plenty of murders, and just might be at the bottom of this tangled web."

Sovern's smile got bigger. Crimes of passion. Now those he understood.

Chapter Forty-four

Scarlett Hayden got off the phone with her old high school friend Pansy Dalrymple, now Glisson. She'd tracked her down through cousin Rachel Gatwood, who kept track of everyone from high school because those class reunions were the highlight of Rachel's year.

Two years out of high school, Pansy had gone to college in Richmond, got married, and moved to Charleston where her husband was from.

After catching up on twenty-five years' worth of life events, Scarlett got to the point and asked about Professor and Mrs. Allan Walter.

According to Pansy, Allan married Jessamine Middleton mostly for her money and family connections.

"Theirs was a marriage of convenience more than anything else," Pansy declared.

"Convenient for whom?" Scarlett asked.

"Supposedly both. He got to play with an endless parade of coeds, plus have access to her money and her circle. Meanwhile, he never complained if she also wished to satisfy her urges outside of their marital bed. The word is that Jessamine likes the occasional nibble of dark meat, if you catch my drift."

Scarlett merely chuckled, then asked, "What about women?"

"There was some speculation, among those who supposedly knew, that she likes young girls, or possibly young boys dressed up as girls."

"What was the reason for the speculation?"

"Well, she took in foster kids. Supposedly all girls. At least they were all dressed like girls. And she would take them to social events with her, quite often in lieu of her husband."

"How young are we talking about?"

"Anywhere from twelve to sixteen or seventeen."

"What did they look like?"

"Well, they were all pretty and they all looked like they hadn't reached puberty yet. What's your interest?"

Scarlett gave her the Reader's Digest version of recent events.

"Oh, my. Why that's just too incredible."

"It is. So don't say a word."

"Oh, I won't."

Scarlett smiled at that, because if this was the same Pansy she knew in high school, the entire state of South Carolina would know about Jessamine by tomorrow morning.

They said goodbye, promising to keep in touch, and ended the call.

This was choice. Scarlett was quite pleased with herself. Now what to do with the information. Blackmail Jessamine? If so, for what reason? She didn't need money. Maybe just dangle it over her head.

"Make her my little puppet," she said.

No, just sit on it for now. She still had her boy toys she needed to talk to.

"Best if I go into battle with all the ammunition I can get."

She began mixing herself a martini, a huge smile on her lips.

Chapter Forty-five

THE LUNCH CROWD AT the Really Good had come and gone. And crowd was an accurate description.

"I guess murder is good for business," Harry mused.

He'd only seen Em briefly, as she'd gotten her lunch to go. A text had come in from Neal, asking him to stop by when he had a chance. And now that things in the shop were quiet, he decided to see what Neal wanted.

He hobbled across the town square to the *Chronicle* office, greeted Rebecca, and made his way to Neal's desk.

"What did you find out?" Harry asked the newspaperman.

"Have a seat. You're going to like this. At least, I did."

He sat, and Neal began.

"I talked to a few people. You remember I said Effie Snyder disappeared for a couple years after college?"

"I do."

"Well, after doing some digging, it seems she went to St. Louis."

"Any particular reason?"

"I talked to a couple reporters I know up there. Old timers, like me, so they know things, and I got them digging. Well, they dug up a hospital record for one Effie Snyder. Seems she gave birth to a baby boy six months after arriving in St. Louis. Found where she stayed, too, after the baby was born. Then two years, one month, and eighteen days after she left Magnolia Bluff, she returns — but with no baby."

"So what happened to him?"

"That's the big mystery. He just vanished."

"Babies don't just vanish. She must've given him away."

"No record of anything official."

"Nobody's ever seen a baby, have they?"

"Nope. No one knew she was pregnant, either. Or I should say, no one is willing to say if they knew she was pregnant."

"So how old would the kid be?"

"Effie's around fifty-three, which would make the kid thirty, or thirty-one."

"Not a kid anymore by a long shot."

"Nope."

"So what do we do with this information?"

"That is a very good question, Thurgood. I'd hazard a guess that if someone brought it up, Effie would deny it. She'd have to. That information would destroy her reputation."

"I suppose it would."

"Hardshell Baptist has a baby out of wedlock? That's an express ticket, first class, to Hell."

"I suppose so. This place is like a time warp."

Neal roared with laughter. When he finally stopped, he said, "You just discover that? Man, you are slow on the uptake, mister."

"Just takes some getting used to. That's all."

"Get used to it. If you plan on stayin'."

"I do. And I guess I will." When Neal didn't say anything, Harry said, "I wonder if she sees him? Has any contact with him?"

"Impossible to know at this point."

"I suppose so. Unless Effie herself says something."

"That hits the nail on the head."

Harry stood. "Thanks for the info. Now we know Effie's dirty little secret. I don't see how it helps us, but it might fit in the picture somewhere."

"That it might, Thurgood. That it might."

Chapter Forty-six

REECE SOVERN STOPPED BY the Really Good and caught Harry just returning from his visit with Neal Holland.

"You have a few minutes? I have a few questions I'd like to ask," Sovern said.

"Sure. Coffee?"

"A cup would be good."

"Harry got Estrelita's attention, said, "Coffee," and held up two fingers. In a moment, she placed two steaming cups before Harry and Sovern.

"So, Reece, what can I do for you?"

"You said we should work together. So here I am. I'm going to tell you what I have thus far, and I would appreciate it if you'd reciprocate. Because I happen to know that there's not a person alive, not Mary Lou Fight, not Terresa Brown, not LouEllen Mueller, or Daphne Leigh, or any one of the Crimson Hat brigade that can hold a candle to Neal Holland for finding out information. And you've been talking to Neal. Working with him I dare say. So—" He leaned back in his chair. "You willing to make a horse trade?"

"Sure. What do you have?"

Reece told Harry what his investigation had uncovered and where he was at trying to piece it all together. When he was done, he watched for Harry's reaction.

"I don't have a whole lot to add, actually," Harry said it last, and went on to round out the picture for Sovern.

When he was done, the detective said, "Well, I'll be damned. A kid?" He shook his head. "That's on par with learning the moon really is made of green cheese. Leave it to Neal to dig up that tidbit. But how does it pertain to the case?"

Harry shrugged. "Don't know that it does."

"I see. Huh. I think I'll have to sleep on that one." Sovern drank coffee. After a moment he said, "You're on the level? That's all you have?"

Harry held up his hands. "That's it. Scout's honor."

Sovern stood. "Thanks, Harry. I appreciate it. This one's a toughie. It's not like we have a murder every week. How much for the coffee?"

"On the house."

"Thanks."

Sovern left the coffee shop, thinking about the Effie Snyder bombshell. As he got in his car, he murmured, "That's a hot bit of news, but I'll be damned if I see any connection to Louisa Middlebrook's death, or the attempt on Mary Lou Fight, or the attempt on Thurgood and the Reverend." He shook his head and started his car.

Chapter Forty-seven

HARRY DECIDED TO HAVE supper at home. He called Ember to see if she would join him, but she had a church meeting.

In the kitchen of the Really Good, he put a steak on the grill and made himself a tossed salad of mixed greens, cucumbers, spring onions, and tomatoes. When the steak was just well done, he put it on a plate and took the food up to his apartment.

To go with the steak, he wanted a bold red wine. In the wine rack were bottles of Texas Syrah, Zinfandel, Malbec, and Lenoir. Since he was in Texas and Lenoir was native to Texas, he opened a bottle of Lenoir and poured himself a glass, then dug into his meal.

With a voice command, the sound of Wagner's *Die Meistersinger* filled his apartment.

He lingered for nearly an hour eating, drinking, and listening to the dazzling music of the opera, and when he was finished, poured himself a cognac and sat in his easy chair, sipping brandy and letting his mind free associate the facts of the case.

However, his mind hadn't done much associating when the buzzer sounded for the street-level door.

Muttering, "Who could that be?" he descended the stairs, looked through the one-way pane of glass, and chuckled. *What in the world does she want?*

He unlocked and opened the door. "Good evening, Scarlett. What brings you to my door?"

"I have some information I think you might like to hear about Jessamine Walter. May I come in?"

"By all means." He held open the door and waved her in.

She entered and followed him up the stairs to the second floor, and into his apartment.

"Let me take your coat."

She took off her car coat, handed it to him, and he hung in on a hook on the back of the door. She deposited herself on the sofa, where she kicked off her shoes, and tucked her legs underneath her.

The pink blouse she was wearing with the dark blue slacks was frilly and lacy and half unbuttoned. Harry surmised she was not wearing a bra.

He asked if she'd like a cognac. She wrinkled her nose, and said, "Martini."

Harry nodded, made her the drink, handed it to her, and sat in his easy chair.

"Smoke your pipe," she commanded.

He arched an eyebrow, while a ghost of a smile touched his lips, "A little bossy, aren't we?" he said.

Scarlett laughed a deep throated laugh, and said, "Sometimes."

Harry filled and lit his pipe. When the cloud of fragrant smoke slowly began to ascend, she took in a deep breath, and cooed, "Man, I like that."

"Okay. What's cooking with Jessamine?"

"I tracked down my friend, Pansy. From high school. She lives in Charleston now. Husband's some big shot doctor, or something. You know, builds better busts." She smiled and sipped her drink.

Harry smiled back.

"Well, she told me a few interesting things about the new queen."

"Such as?"

Scarlett took a big swallow of her martini, ate an olive, and told Harry her news. When she was finished, she said, "What do you make of that?" And took another big swallow of her drink, followed by the second olive.

Harry raised his eyebrows. "I guess it shows we all have our dirty little secrets. Our forbidden pleasures. The ones we're too ashamed of to put on public display."

Scarlett licked her lips. "I'm not done, Harry, baby."

"Enlighten me."

"One of my boy toys told me this afternoon that Terrell Williams, our star halfback on the college football team, has been 'doin' one of the history professor's wives."

"Did he say which one?"

"He didn't want to say at first, but he succumbed to persuasion." Scarlett's smile dripped seduction.

"And?"

"Why, our new queen, of course." She finished her martini and held up the glass indicating she wanted a refill.

Harry obliged and returned to his chair.

"Well? Is that useful, or what?" Scarlett demanded.

"I think it's useful. Congratulations on your resourcefulness. And thank you for sharing."

"Now, will you make love to me? It would be a much nicer way to say thank you."

"I can't, Scarlett. I don't love you."

"You know what I mean. Throw me on your bed and take me. Let's rumple the sheets."

"I think you'd best go home."

She stood, threw the martini glass at Harry, and shouted, "Damn you, damn you, damn you. I hate you, Harry Thurgood." She grabbed her coat and stormed out of his apartment.

Harry walked to the stairwell and got there in time to see and hear the door slam shut. He locked the door, returned to his living room, and cleaned up the mess.

He made himself a Corpse Reviver No. 1 and returned to his easy chair. The information was good. In fact, it just might be the piece that would put order to the mess they had on their hands.

"Too bad I had to lose a friend over it."

Chapter Forty-eight

HARRY SIPPED HIS DRINK. The question, though, was what to do with the information? Should he call Reece and give it to him right away? Should he sit on it? Pass it on to Neal? Confront Jessamine directly? Or maybe he should meet with this Terrell person and clarify exactly what was going on.

He picked up his phone and told it to call Ember, and in a moment he heard her voice saying, "No, you can't come over."

"I wasn't going to ask if I could."

"Good. And no, I'm not going to your place. In fact, I'm not going anywhere."

"Okay. I take it this is a bad time?"

"I just made myself a cup of hot tea, and I'm luxuriating in my bubble bath."

"Luxuriating, eh? Well, God forbid I interrupt your luxuriating. Call me when you've been fully luxuriated."

"Dream on, Mister."

"Beautiful dreamer, wake unto—" Harry realized Ember had terminated the call.

He chuckled and continued singing. "Starlight and dewdrops are waiting for thee." Then he sighed. "Oh, Em, we could make such beautiful music together. How can I break through that ice field with which you've surrounded yourself?"

Glass in hand, he got up, and stood by the window. East Main Street was lit by amber-colored streetlights and completely deserted. The sky was overcast. He'd be seeing no blue moon tonight.

He finished his drink, made himself a new one, and sat in his easy chair. While sipping his cocktail, he gently rocked. He forced his mind to turn from Ember Cole to Jessamine Walter. A woman who apparently liked the occasional black partner and was either into young women or boys dressed up as young women.

"What messed up worlds we make for ourselves," he said out loud. "Whatever happened to getting married, growing old together, and experiencing all the different phases of love with that one person?"

A great big sigh escaped from Harry's lips. "Maybe I'm a man born out of time."

He rocked, sipped his drink, and rocked some more. His mind ran over the data he, Ember, Neal, and Reece had collected. This new bit concerning Jessamine was every bit as big as that concerning Effie.

"But do they fit? Do they even matter? And if they do matter, where do they fit?" He took a swallow of his drink and continued his musing. "It probably all fits somewhere, somehow. I just need another pair of eyes to help me make sense of it all. Who, though, should I ask?"

Chapter Forty-nine

SCARLETT HAYDEN WAS LIVID. "Talk about ungrateful. What the hell does Ember Cole have that I don't? I bet Harry Thurgood *is* into boys. Just wait until *that* gets around town. It'll be really good." She barked a harsh laugh at her joke. "And as for that skinny bitch, I'm going to take her down."

She pulled over to the side of the road and told her phone to call Jessamine.

The voice at the other end said, "What do you want? Do you realize what time it is?"

"You and I need to meet. Now."

"I hardly think so."

"You won't be saying that once the town finds out about your sexual peccadilloes."

There was silence on the other end.

"The park," Scarlett commanded. "Ten minutes. Don't be late."

***

Scarlett parked her Land Rover next to the silver Jaguar and smiled. She had Jessamine right where she wanted her.

She stepped out of the big SUV, scanned the area, and saw a person sitting on a bench. From the hairdo, she knew the person was Jessamine. She walked over to the bench, sat on the opposite end.

"What do you want, Scarlett?"

"My, my. You aren't even going to ask me what I know?"

"Will it make any difference?"

"I don't know. It might. Tell you what, why don't I tell you what I know. That way, I'll get less argument."

"Suit yourself."

"I always wondered why I could never get Terrell to pay me a visit, and why Darryl called me 'Jessamine' one afternoon. Now I know. But how is it you get to keep Terrell all to yourself? That isn't fair, you know. Share and share alike."

Jessamine said nothing.

"I suppose it doesn't matter. I have plenty of toys to play with. You keep Terrell. I'll let you."

"Slut."

"My, my. Don't you think that is the pot calling the kettle black?" She chuckled at the pun.

From the other end of the bench there was only silence, so Scarlett continued. "Now what I can't figure out is do you like girls, or just boys dressed up as girls? Oh, heavens. Maybe it's both. Is it?"

"You've made your point. What do you want?"

"Oh, that's simple. From now on, you simply say, 'How high, Ms. Scarlett? How high do you want me to jump?' Do we understand each other?"

"Yes."

"Oh, one other thing. Ember Cole is not to get a crimson hat."

Jessamine said not a word.

"Well?"

"I heard you."

"Good. Sleep well." Scarlett stood, blew Jessamine a kiss, and started for her car.

She was halfway there when she felt the burning, and the shove, and heard the firecracker, loud in the night. She stumbled. *God, that hurts*, she thought, as she fell, and was swallowed up by the moonless night.

Chapter Fifty

EMBER COLE HAD JUST gotten out of the tub when she heard the first siren. It was followed quickly by a second.

"Wonder what's going on?" she muttered while toweling herself. "Hope it's not another murder."

She pulled on her pajamas and slipped into her robe. "I wonder what Harry wanted?" She picked up her phone, put it down, picked it up, and told it to call Harry.

After three rings, he answered. "You hear the sirens?"

"I did."

"Any idea as to what's going on?"

"I thought you angels knew these things."

"It was a test."

"Yeah, right. I'm beginning to think you're a fallen angel."

"Hey, we angels do have feelings, you know."

"Sorry. I'm calling because you apparently had something important to tell me."

"I do."

"So tell me."

"Can't we meet?"

"No, we can't. I'm in my jammies heading for bed."

"Very well, then, I guess the phone will have to do."

"Yes, it will." Ember listened as Harry told her what he'd found out about Effie and Jessamine. When he was done, all she could say was, "Wow."

"Wow, indeed."

"But how does all of this with Effie and Jessamine fit in with Louisa's death, running down Mary Lou, and the attempt to run us down?"

"Don't know. That's the kicker. It all fits together, but none of us can figure out how."

"Are you sure? Are you sure it fits together?"

"Aw, c'mon, Em. Of course it fits together."

"Okay, if you say so."

"You're not convinced."

"No, I'm not."

"All of this has to do with you. If we take you out of the equation, then none of this makes sense. There'd be no reason to kill Louisa or try to kill Mary Lou. Effie wouldn't think she had to protect you, and Jessamine wouldn't be making a power play for the Hats in order to get you in. You are the epicenter, but just how everything fits together isn't making itself apparent. How the puzzle comes together to tell us who's the killer is eluding us."

Ember thought a moment, before saying, "Okay. I can see that I'm at the center of all this, and I agree with you that how all the pieces come together isn't at all clear. What is clear is that Mary Lou decided the church needed a new pastor. What also seems clear is that the Hats were supposed to provide her with information. What isn't clear is why Louisa was targeted first? Why not Mary Lou? If Effie is the killer, and she's trying to protect me, why kill Louisa? And why try to run us down?"

"Or maybe just run me down."

"Maybe, but that doesn't make any sense either. You're not a threat."

"I didn't think so, but maybe in her addled mind I am."

"Possible, I suppose. But that still doesn't account for Jessamine. Is she just an opportunist taking advantage of the situation? Or did she help create the situation in order to take advantage of it? And would she kill someone just to take over the Hats? That really seems farfetched."

"Although, if this info about Jessamine is true, maybe she's being driven by unholy desires."

Ember laughed. "Unholy desires? Listen to you. Straight out of the Middle Ages."

"I'm an angel, remember?"

"Yeah? Well, how many of you jokers can dance on the head of a pin?"

"Very funny."

"And no, I don't think 'unholy desires' is sufficient motive to kill someone."

"But you do agree that you are the center of this drama, right?"

"That part does make sense. It's about the only thing that makes any sense."

"I agree with you there."

"Well, Mr. Angel, I need to get my beauty sleep. Lord knows I need it."

"That's not true, Em. You're very beautiful. You may need sleep, but it won't improve how beautiful you are."

"C'mon, Harry. I'm—"

"Ember Cole, you are the most beautiful woman in the world."

"You do remember we're friends, right?"

"Yes, I do. Does that mean I can't call you beautiful?"

"No, but I wish you wouldn't."

"Why?"

"Because it will take us to a place we can't go."

"Okay. But now that I've told you, just remember it. Because it's what I think every time I see you."

"Harry, you're making this difficult. Please don't. Please?"

"All right. Forget I said anything. Better?"

"Yes. Better. Who else knows what you told me?"

"Only you have all of the information."

"Maybe we should meet with Reece and Neal and fill them in. Definitely Reece, otherwise we could be in hot water."

"I agree."

"Meanwhile, Mr. Angel, we can sleep on it."

They said goodnight and ended the call.

Ember set her alarm, turned off the light, and crawled into bed. Wilbur was already curled up on the pillow next to hers.

The night light cast a soft glow, and Ember studied the shadows on the ceiling.

"I don't know, Wilbur. This sure is a mess. But let's say that Jessamine, because of 'unholy desires'..." She giggled, and just as quickly got serious again. "Jessamine kills Mary Lou's staunchest supporter and tries to kill Mary Lou but fails. She does, however, force her off the playing field, and by doing so she can take over the Hats. She then begins buttering me up by offering me membership in the Hats where we'll have lots of opportunity to be together. Then at some point..."

Ember yawned. "Seems a bit farfetched, if you ask me. Don't you think so, Wilbur? Thought so. But if instead of Jessamine, the culprit is Effie. She kills Louisa to exact revenge for being dumped as Louisa's friend when she joined the Hats, and at the same time tries to get rid of Mary Lou because she wants to protect me. She gets rid of the two people who have upset the apple cart of her world. Now that makes a whole lot more sense to me."

Another yawn, and Ember turned on her side. "But how does Harry fit into all of this?" She turned the question over in her mind. "For Jessamine, the reason would be to get rid of the competition. That would make a lot of sense. But why would Effie want to get rid of Harry? He's certainly not competition from her perspective." She yawned, and then she saw the light bulb come on. "Of course, Effie sees Harry as a corrupting influence. Someone who will take me, the Lord's Anointed, away from her just as Mary Lou took away Louisa.

Ember nodded. "That makes perfect sense. But what about that car? It was going to hit both of us. Both Harry *and* me. Either we were both the target, or the driver didn't recognize one of us. And if that's the case, then the driver probably wasn't Jessamine or Effie. But if he or she wasn't one of them, who was it?"

She repeated, "Who was it?" and drifted off to sleep.

Chapter Fifty-one

THE PHONE WAS RINGING. Actually a snippet of "The Ride of the Valkyries" was playing. Harry silenced it. The ringtone started up again.

"What the hell?" He looked at the screen. Local number. 3:47 am. *Might be important.* He shrugged and answered with a "Hello."

"Neal Holland here, Thurgood."

"Is it important?"

"It's all important. The task is to figure out which page it belongs on. And this is front page material."

"Okay. Shoot."

"That's it exactly. Someone shot Scarlett Hayden."

"Good God." Harry sat up. "Is she dead?"

"No, she isn't. Twenty-five caliber bullet did a number on her right kidney, and she lost a lot of blood. But as of fifteen minutes ago, she was still breathing. Reece Sovern will be meeting up with you sooner rather than later because she uttered one word in her moment of consciousness before surgery. And that word was, 'Thurgood.' Any idea why she'd mention your name?"

"She stopped by my place after supper. Told me some juicy gossip about Jessamine, then left."

"You didn't shoot her, by chance, did you?"

Harry rolled his eyes, not that Neal could see. "If I did, it wouldn't be with a twenty-five."

"A twenty-five can kill you just as dead as a forty-four magnum. Just makes a smaller hole is all."

"I suppose you're right. Nevertheless, give me a three-fifty-seven magnum or a forty-five any day. Thanks for the info."

"Wait. Aren't you going to tell me the gossip?"

He obliged the newspaperman, and Neal's only comment before ringing off was, "Well, I'll be a son of a gun."

Harry put the phone down, and his head back on the pillow. But he was too wide awake, and his eyes refused to close in sleep.

After tossing and turning for a quarter hour, he got up, showered, dressed, and went downstairs to the shop. He made coffee and started the wood-fired grill, on which he made himself ham and eggs. Finishing just as Miguel came in the back door.

"Good morning, Mr. Thurgood."

"Morning, Miguel. Coffee's on. Just making myself some breakfast. Couldn't sleep."

"Very good, Mr. Thurgood. Thank you for getting the fire going."

"You're welcome."

Harry took his plate and cup of coffee to his corner table, snagging a day old doughnut on the way, and sat.

A fork of egg had just made it to his mouth when there was pounding on the front door.

"I bet that's Sovern," Harry muttered, while getting up and crossing the floor. He peeked through the blinds, recognized the cigar, and let the investigator in.

"I suppose you've heard the news by now, Thurgood."

"Which news? Coffee? Breakfast?"

"Come to think of it that sounds good."

"What'll you have?"

"Eggs, sausage, and toast."

Harry called out Sovern's request to Miguel and poured the investigator a cup of coffee. They sat at Harry's table.

"Okay, Thurgood, I'm guessing you've heard the news."

"I've heard lots of news. Which item are you referring to?"

"Your good friend, Scarlett Hayden. Somebody shot her. They probably would've finished her off if it wasn't for Phineas Henry. He was out walking his dog. Heard the shot, dropped the leash, and the dog took off. Apparently scared off the shooter. By the time Henry showed up, the dog was standing guard by the Hayden woman. He called emergency, and she's in intensive care after the surgeon extracted the bullet."

"That's just plain awful. Robbery?"

"Nope. This was something else. You wouldn't happen to know why she said your name before she went into surgery, would you?"

"No, I don't. But she did stop by my place to give me some gossip she'd dug up."

"You care to enlighten me?"

"Sure." And Harry told Sovern what Scarlett had told him.

"Well, I'll be..."

Miguel brought out Sovern's breakfast. The detective nodded his thanks and speared a sausage. He took a bite, chewed, and swallowed.

"What do you make of that, Thurgood? A woman having the hots for your girlfriend?"

"She's not my girlfriend."

"Yeah, right." The detective drank coffee.

"I just find it difficult to believe that a person would kill someone just because of lust. You get turned down, just find someone else. There are plenty of fish in the sea."

"Let me clue you in, Thurgood. There's no creature on God's green earth as depraved as a human being. If you believe that rubbish about the innate goodness of man, then I bet I can convince you Grant surrendered at Appomattox Courthouse. Why do you think there are all those rules in the Good Book to keep us in line? It's because we're perverse and degenerate, that's why."

Sovern ate his breakfast, while Harry took a bite of doughnut and played with the ham and eggs. He chewed on what the police investigator had said.

When Sovern had finished eating, Harry refilled their coffee cups.

The detective asked, when Harry was once again seated, "So you think she said your name so you'd tell me what she told you?"

"I think so. It might also be her way of telling us who shot her."

"That it might. Well, I'm off to talk to Jessamine. I'll send someone to round up this college kid she's been playing house with."

"Might want to check his car."

"Good idea, Thurgood. How much for breakfast?"

"On the house."

"That's not how to make money but thank you."

Sovern got up and left the coffee shop.

Harry finished eating his ham and eggs, collected the dishes, took them back to the kitchen, all the while wondering if humanity was truly as bad as Sovern thought.

Who are you kidding, Harry, of course it is. You've had your own run ins with depravity.

"That I have," he said under his breath as he made his way back to his table, snaring another doughnut on the way.

"Ember and her fellow persons of the cloth sure have their work cut out for them."

Chapter Fifty-two

Ember sat at the far end of the counter, eating her breakfast sandwich. The Really Good was actually semi-busy. Further down the counter a couple men were seated drinking coffee and reading the paper. Four tables were occupied. A woman sat alone by the door and was having a quiet conversation with someone on her phone. Two women chatted over coffee at a second. A husband and wife occupied a third, and Fergus was at the fourth in the far corner.

Harry, Estrelita, and Jack were kept busy. Not to mention Miguel in the kitchen.

I suppose this is a good thing, Ember mused. *Harry needs to start making money from this place. I'd hate to see him have to close.*

After a moment or two, she also admitted she didn't want him to leave town. He was her best friend. And it had been a long time since she had a best friend.

Harry sat on the stool next to her. "I might have to hire another waitress."

"I don't think that's PC."

Harry frowned, then said, "They are waiters or waitresses. Although I might tolerate server."

Ember laughed. "You can be so old-fashioned at times."

"There's nothing wrong with being old-fashioned. In fact, I think it's rather charming."

"You do, huh?"

"I do."

"Well, I came up with something else that's charming."

"And what's that?"

"I think our culprit is Effie. She has the clearest and most believable motivation: she's protecting me out of some misguided religious belief and eliminating all the threats."

"And how am I a threat?"

"You like me. We're friends. You are a bad worldly influence, just like Mary Lou was to Louisa. You might just take me away from her, as Mary Lou did Louisa."

"Yes, I guess that makes sense. But did she have the means and the opportunity?"

"Well, she does have a car. And cars aren't that difficult to get a hold of."

"Have you considered that the other night that car would've hit both of us?"

"Yes. What it tells me is that Effie wasn't the driver. The person recognized you, but not me."

"It does make sense, Em. I think you've nailed it. Now we just have to figure out how she did it."

Chapter Fifty-three

REECE SOVERN TURNED ONTO Sandalwood Drive, heading for Jessamine Walter's place. He was three houses down, when he saw her Jaguar pull out of the drive.

He flipped on the lights, turned to block her lane, and was getting out of the car, when the Jaguar plowed into his sedan.

***

"Mr. Thurgood," Miguel said, "John Paul is here with the delivery. He wants to ask you a question."

Harry told Ember not to leave and walked back to the delivery door at the rear of the kitchen.

"Good morning, John Paul."

"Mornin', Mr. Thurgood, sir. Elder Smythe wants to know if you're interested in any goose?"

"Goose? I haven't had goose in ages. How many does he have and at what price?"

"He has three. Cleaned and with the feathers taken off. He'd like forty dollars for each bird."

"That's a bit pricey, but then the last time I bought goose was years ago."

"Elder Smythe said finding goose is mighty hard, and he's planning on selling them for sixty dollars each."

"So I'm getting a deal. Is that it?" Harry smiled.

"Yes, sir. He told me to say that."

"Okay, John Paul. I'll take the three."

"I'll bring them this afternoon."

Harry watched John Paul get in the old pickup truck and drive off. Not for the first time, he thought the young man looked familiar. That he'd seen him someplace else. He shook his head and returned to the front of the restaurant.

"What was that all about?" Ember asked.

"Apparently, Elder Smythe is slaughtering a few of his geese. Wanted to know if I was interested at forty bucks a bird."

"Kind of pricey."

"Goose is difficult to find, and I like it."

"So you bought them."

"I did."

Ember shook her head, and playfully punched Harry's shoulder. "Softy. But I'm sure Hezekiah appreciates the business."

"S'pose so."

"Did you know Primitive Baptist elders don't get paid by their church? They have to support themselves?"

"Really? Didn't know that. No wonder he appreciates my business."

"You're helping him pay his bills."

"Do you know much about Elder Smythe?"

"Not really. I've visited a few times, and I buy produce and fruit from him. The Primitives kind of stick to themselves."

"Know anything about John Paul?"

"Just that he works for Hezekiah. The Smythes hired John Paul after their kids moved away. They provide him with room and board and a little bit of cash. Apparently, Effie somehow knows John Paul and asked Hezekiah to take him on as a favor.

Harry thought a moment, then nodded. "That's who he reminds me of."

"Who reminds you of whom?"

"John Paul reminds me of Effie."

Ember scrunched up her face, then shook her head, "Haven't seen him in a while."

"You doing anything right now?"

"Just going to work on my sermon."

"Want to go for a ride?"

"Where to?"

"To talk to Elder Hezekiah Smythe."

Chapter Fifty-four

REECE SOVERN GROANED. HE was lying on the street. His leg hurt. His head hurt. In the distance he heard a siren.

He sat up. A wave of nausea swept over him, and he fought the urge to throw up.

The siren got louder. He tried to think what happened. A woman appeared and asked him if he was all right.

"I don't know."

"The ambulance is on its way."

"What happened?"

"I don't know. I just heard the bang, saw that Jessamine's car had hit yours, and that you were on the ground."

The siren was very loud and suddenly stopped. In a moment, a paramedic stooped down and began asking Sovern questions.

***

Harry and Ember drove out to the Primitive Baptist church, which was a couple miles to the northeast of Magnolia Bluff. Next to the church building was a ten acre piece of land that belonged to Elder Hezekiah Smythe. The five acres on which the church building sat had once been part of Smythe's parcel, but he'd given it to the church, which he'd started, as a gift.

"Know anything about the church?" Harry asked.

"Hezekiah started it thirty, thirty-five years ago. The congregation numbers twenty-five or thirty, if I recall. He's a good preacher and has a beautiful singing voice. Some of the conservative Southern Baptists have joined, although I'm not sure everyone buys Smythe's hardcore Calvinist theology."

"That's a bit over my head. The upshot is if you're looking for a very conservative church, then this is the place to be."

"You got it."

Harry pulled into the drive and parked his car. He and Ember got out, walked up to the door, and knocked. In a moment, a woman answered. "Oh, Miss Cole. Good morning." The woman gave him a questioning look.

"I'm Harry Thurgood. You must be Hannah. I do business with Elder Smythe."

"Oh, we meet at last. Yes, I'm Hannah Smythe, Hezekiah's wife." She offered her hand and Harry took it, shaking hands with her. "Hezekiah tells me you are one of his best customers."

"Hard to beat good fruit, meat, and vegetables."

"We're here to see Elder Smythe, if he's in," Ember said.

"He's working in the strawberries. Out back."

"I think I remember how to get there," Ember said.

"You can't miss him. I'd take you back, but I'm in the middle of baking and making dinner."

Harry and Ember said goodbye and walked out behind the house.

"I recall Smythe saying he has a fig orchard as his main cash crop and supplements with strawberries, blackberries, and jujubes," Harry said.

"That's where most of his cash comes from. He gets some extra selling chicken, eggs, goat meat, vegetables, and now he's adding geese."

"I mostly get eggs, fresh figs in season, and berries. Occasionally vegetables and a chicken or two. All good quality."

"Hard to beat fresh."

They followed the path out to the orchard. On the way, they saw John Paul cleaning geese, and waved. He waved back and returned to his work.

When they were some thirty or forty feet away, Elder Smythe saw them and stood. He was a tall man and lean. He had luxuriously thick and wavy brown hair even though Harry guessed him to be pushing sixty.

"Mr. Thurgood, Pastor Cole, good morning. The strawberry crop promises to be a good one. The Lord is good. How may I help you?"

They all shook hands, followed by Harry asking what the Baptist minister could tell them about John Paul.

"Miss Effie Snyder brought him to us some seven years ago, askin' if we could give him room and board in exchange for work. He's rather slow, you see, and Miss Snyder wanted a good God-fearin' environment for him.

"Hannah and I talked it over and decided to take him in, seein' as our own children had all decided to move on. We asked if he was family because his name's also Snyder. She said he was a distant cousin and didn't seem too inclined to tell us anymore. We didn't want to press her for particulars, some things are best left in the past, if you know what I mean."

Harry and Ember nodded their agreement.

"The boy seemed nice enough, very polite and mannerly, and we know Miss Snyder is a God-fearin' woman, so Hannah and I said we'd try him for a month."

"He obviously worked out," Harry said.

"Yes, he did. He's a good worker and he loves the Lord. He's not ours, but we treat him as if he was."

"Does Effie visit him?" Ember asked.

"She does. About once a week. Bought him a phone and talks to him nearly every day. May I ask why you're interested in John Paul?"

"I'm looking for some help, but I see you'd be lost without him," Harry prevaricated. "You probably have enough work for two of him."

"Indeed, I do, Mr. Thurgood. But it's good to know he made a favorable impression."

"Thank you, Elder Smythe. We'll let you get back to your work."

"May the Lord be with you."

"And also with you," Ember replied.

On the way back to the car, Harry said, "Now we talk to Effie. Because we both know she has no distant cousins."

"At least none she's aware of or told anyone about."

Chapter Fifty-five

AFTER THREE HOURS, REECE Sovern said enough was enough and left the hospital. He learned that Jessamine Walter had been treated for air bag-related cuts, abrasions, burns, and bruises, and then released.

Officer Dick Schreiber gave the detective a lift back out to the Walter residence. However, there was no answer to the incessant ringing of the doorbell, and after five minutes, Sovern gave up and had Schreiber drive him back to the police station.

His first stop was to see Chief Jager.

"The hospital isn't too happy you just up and left," the Chief said when Sovern poked his head in and asked if he had a minute.

"Probably not. But I've work to do."

The Chief waved him in. "There's a report on your desk. Hagedorn came up empty handed on Terrell Williams. Seems he may have done a runner."

Sovern nodded. "I was just at Jessamine Walter's place. Didn't answer her door. I'd like you to okay keeping a watch on the house and to bring her in for questioning when she shows up. I'm tired of being Mr. Nice Guy."

"You got it. Anything else?"

"Some aspirin for this damn headache."

"You should go home. Take the rest of the day off. I'll call you if anything turns up."

"Won't get any rest. I'll just be chewing on this case like a piece of tough steak. Might as well sit at my desk."

Jager shrugged. "Suit yourself."

On the way to his office, Sovern snagged a cup of coffee for himself. He entered his little home away from home, looked around, sat behind his desk, and, wincing from the pain in his sore leg, put his feet up on the corner.

He sipped coffee. It was black and it was hot. And it tasted like crap compared to Thurgood's java. But right now, hot was all he cared for. He closed his eyes and his thoughts riffled through the data on the case. Or maybe cases.

Jessamine and the college kid were MIA. A possible indicator they were guilty of something. As soon as he could talk to the Hayden woman, he'd know if Jessamine was the trigger puller or not.

But were those two, the Walter woman and the football player, were they the ones responsible for killing Louisa Middlebrook, running down Mary Lou Fight, and attempting to run down Thurgood and the Reverend? If so, the sooner he got them off the streets, the better it would be for everyone in Magnolia Bluff.

***

After grabbing a couple sandwiches from the kitchen of the Really Good, Harry and Ember drove over to the Methodist Church.

"Effie is often there answering the phone, opening mail, and taking care of the day to day," Ember said. After a moment, she added, "I'm going to miss her a lot if she has to go away."

"If she killed Louisa, I can see her falling on her sword to spare her son."

"If he is her son, yes, I can see that."

"C'mon, Em, he looks too much like her not to be."

Ember sighed. "This is all so sad. People are sure messed up, not to mention the hard lives so many live."

"Don't you believe in original sin?"

"I don't know, Harry. I know the Bible talks about it, but I just can't bring myself to go there. I want to believe in the goodness of people."

"So you think Adam and Eve were, say, symbolic? A picture of each of us?"

"I guess. Something like that. Although that isn't what the Articles of Religion teach."

"All I know is that there are good people, bad people, and a whole lot in between."

Harry pulled up in front of the Methodist Church and parked on the street. They got out and entered the building, heading to the back where the offices were located. Effie Snyder was at the church secretary's desk tapping away at the computer keyboard.

She looked up as they approached the desk. "Hello, Reverend Cole. Mr. Thurgood." Her face focused on Ember. "I put your mail on your desk."

"Do you mind joining us in my office?" Ember said. "We'd like to talk to you."

Effie hesitated, and then stood. "Both of you?"

Ember nodded, and said, "Yes."

Harry watched Effie closely. Her face was blank, registering no emotion. She simply turned and walked into Ember's office.

Effie sat on the sofa, while Ember and Harry sat on chairs facing her. On the way over to the church, the two had agreed that Ember should do the talking. Harry only joining in if needed.

"This is going to be very difficult for me, Effie, but I need to know if what I'm about to say is true."

"Does he have to be here?"

"No, I don't, if it will make you feel more comfortable talking with Reverend Cole."

"There are things a woman doesn't wish to talk about in front of a man."

Harry stood. "I'll wait outside."

"Thanks, Harry," Ember said.

He left.

***

The two women looked at each other for a few moments, before Ember said, "Would you join me in prayer?"

"Say what you've come to say, Reverend Cole. If we need to pray, we can do so afterwards."

"Okay. I won't drag it out. And I'm not judging you, Effie, because the Lord knows I am a sinner saved by grace."

"We all are who trust in the Lord Jesus."

"We are. If what I've heard is true, you got pregnant in college, went away and had the child, and then sometime later returned to Magnolia Bluff. Did you give him up for adoption?"

Effie bowed her head, and for the longest time said nothing. Ember simply waited. At last, Effie spoke.

"Why are you asking me this? If it's true, that was a long time ago, and the Lord has forgiven my sin."

"It's not true?"

Effie looked at the clasped hands in her lap. "The Lord is merciful. He saves sinners. He forgives them their sin."

"Yes, He does. But we don't always forgive ourselves, do we?"

Effie lifted her head and she and Ember looked into each other's eyes.

"Forgiving ourselves is the hardest part, isn't it, Effie? I know because I haven't forgiven myself either. Is the story true?"

Ember watched the woman bow her head and stare at the hands twisting in her lap, and then heard the words, "I can't lie to the Lord's Anointed. I can't compound my sin." Effie's voice changed ever so slightly. "But you can't tell the truth either. What you did was wrong. It was vile. No one can know." Silence, then, "But God knows, and now His Anointed knows. Oh, God, can I never be free from this sin? Once. Only once. He said he loved me, but it was a lie. And now I'm the lie. A living lie. Oh, God. Oh, God." And Effie began to wail.

Ember sat next to the older woman, put her arms around her, and hugged her. Effie seemed to melt into her, but suddenly stiffened, and stood.

"Lies. It's all lies. And now you, too, are against me."

"No, No, I'm..."

Effie tore open the door and stormed out of the office. Ember ran after her but stopped when she saw Harry.

"I take it the chat didn't go well," he said.

"Not only did it not go well, I think she's mentally ill."

Chapter Fifty-six

JESSAMINE WALTER LOOKED AT the motel room and sniffed her disgust. The room smelled musty. The small desk was scarred with cigarette burns. The chair seat was torn. The dark green carpet by the door was worn down to the backing. A Welcome mat didn't quite cover the spot. The wallpaper was a dark blue stripe pattern and was peeling in two of the corners by the ceiling. And the bathroom... She shuddered.

There were stains on the bedspread, and Jessamine hesitated to sit. However, she decided she could always buy new clothes and sat on the edge of the bed.

Her immediate concern was a car. She needed one and needed one badly. Reece Sovern had been there for one reason and one reason only. That bitch was alive and had told the police who shot her.

What a mess. She needed a drink. God, she needed a drink. Charmaine had promised to come back and help her buy a car. Hopefully, she'd bring a bottle of Pimm's. At this point, though, anything would do.

She just hoped that idiot Terrell had left town. Gone back to whatever ghetto he'd come from.

But where was she going to go? She needed a new identity and wondered if there were people who, for a hundred thousand dollars could give you a new identity. Like on that TV show. If there were, how did one find them?

Why, why, why did Allan have to take a position in that godforsaken town? Why? Life had been good in Charleston. Very good.

She got up and pulled the curtain aside to peek out the window. The parking lot had four cars in it. The asphalt was broken and weeds were growing through the holes and cracks.

The nearest town was three miles away. She returned to the bed and sat and waited. Hoping Charmaine would return soon.

***

Reece Sovern stood next to Scarlett Hayden's hospital bed. She opened her eyes. Her voice was weak and hoarse. "Sorry I can't offer you anything."

"Understandable. Do you want to make a statement? Did Thurgood shoot you?"

"Harry?" She started to laugh, winced, and thought better of it. "Hell, no. It was Jessamine Walter."

"Jessamine?"

She nodded. "I guess I need to be more careful who I try to blackmail. Never for the life of me would I guess *she* had a gun."

"She shot you because you were trying to blackmail her?"

"I think that's what I just said. Although, I doubt she'll willingly corroborate my story."

"We can't find her. Would you know where she might have gone?"

"No. Check with Charmaine Adler. If anybody knows where she is, it will be her."

"Thanks. I'll be back for that statement."

Scarlett smiled. "You know where to find me."

***

Effie Snyder slammed on the brakes and skidded to a stop in the driveway of the home of Elder and Mrs. Smythe. She got out of the car, ran to the door, and pounded on it. The door opened and Effie was looking at Hannah Smythe.

"Where's John Paul?" Effie demanded.

"He's out back in the vegetable garden."

"Promise me you'll take good care of him. Promise me you'll treat him like your own son."

"What's the matter..."

"Promise me!"

"Why, sure Miss Snyder. Hezekiah..."

That was good enough for Effie. She ran back to the vegetable garden. John Paul was hoeing. She ran up to him and threw her arms around him.

"Oh, my boy, my darling boy."

"Momma, what are you doing here?"

She pulled away to look at the young man. "Remember, John Paul, remember I love you and will always love you. If good ever came from evil, you are that good. Just remember: I love you and even if I'm in Hell, I will defy the Devil to watch over you."

"Sure, Momma, I'll remember."

She kissed his cheek, smiled at him, and walked away. As she was about to go around the house, she turned, saw him looking at her. She smiled, waved, and ran to her car.

Chapter Fifty-seven

JESSAMINE LOOKED AT HER watch. The time was only four minutes later than the last time she's looked.

Where was she? Charmaine should have been here by now.

"I need a car," she said, her voice barely audible. "I need to go far away."

For some reason, a verse, and not one she wanted to think about, drifted into her mind, and she said it out loud, "Be sure your sin will find you out."

Everything had been going so well. She'd taken over the Crimson Hat Society. She was going to have that cute Ember Cole in the group and near her all the time. Allan provided the money. Well, some money, at least. It was people, like Terrell and Ember, who made her feel alive and wanted, and gave her some pleasure in what was an otherwise horribly boring existence.

There was a knock on the door. She jumped up, opened the door, and found herself looking at the face of Reece Sovern.

She slapped him hard on the cheek and slammed the door closed, throwing the deadbolt.

The voice of the police investigator came through the door loud and clear. "Open the door, Mrs. Walter. We know what happened. You have to come with us."

What was she going to do? This was it. A lifetime of humiliation. How could she bear it?

"Open the door, Mrs. Walter, or we will break it down."

Jessamine picked up her purse, took out the small, flat, black, semi-automatic pistol. She put the muzzle against the soft flesh behind her chin and pulled the trigger.

***

On the way to the far side of Burnet Reservoir, Effie had stopped at a gas station, and soaked a length of cloth in gasoline. The manager was none too happy about the gas she spilled on the ground. He'd yelled at her, but she ignored him and drove off.

Now, she was parked alongside the road and had a beautiful view of Magnolia Bluff. Virtually her whole life had been spent there.

She prayed and quoted the verse, "He was a man of sorrows and acquainted with grief." That man was her Lord.

"I'm sorry I haven't been the best servant. I tried, I tried real hard. Please forgive me this one last sin. 'As in man came death, so also by man came the resurrection from the dead. As in Adam all die, even so in Christ shall all be made alive.' I'm holding You to that. Please, Jesus, don't fail me."

Effie got out of the car, stuffed the gasoline soaked rag in the filler tube, lit it, and got back into the car.

She started singing.

Rock of Ages cleft for me,
Let me hide myself in Thee.
Let the water and the blood
From Thy riven side which flowed,
Be of sin the double cure,
Cleanse me from its guilt and power.

From across Burnet Reservoir people wondered what was on fire.

Chapter Fifty-eight

A WEEK HAD PASSED since the fateful events of that Tuesday afternoon. At a table in the Really Good Wood-Fired Coffee Shop sat Harry Thurgood, Ember Cole, Neal Holland, and Reece Sovern.

Sovern took the cigar out of his mouth and drank coffee. "We finally tracked down Terrell Williams."

"Where'd you find him?" Neal asked.

"Home. Sussex Heights. A ritzy suburb of Louisville. Father's some kind of a contractor. That kid needed a scholarship like I need a hangover. Nothing's fair. Nothing."

"So what happened?" Neal pressed.

"Nothing. He's working with his father and will return to school next year. Father said he was needed at home. Emergency. That's why he left the college so abruptly. The kid didn't admit to anything and the father started talking lawyer. Jager said it wasn't worth our time to pursue it. So that's that."

"Too bad," Neal said. "I'm sure there's a story there."

"You're welcome to it, Holland." Sovern stuck the cigar back in his mouth, after drinking coffee.

"I talked with Scarlett Hayden," Neal said, "but she wouldn't tell me anything. Said that was in the past. I reminded her of Faulkner. She just laughed and offered me a drink."

"She's home?" Ember asked.

"Yep," Neal said. "Discharged four days ago."

She turned to the police investigator. "Are the cases closed?"

"Technically, no. Well, the assault on the Hayden woman is. Jessamine Walter's little twenty-five is what was used to put a bullet in her. So that's a wrap. But the Middlebrook murder, and the attempt on Mary Lou Fight, well..." He shrugged. "No one confessed, and Effie Snyder's car, if it had any evidence, it was destroyed in the fire."

"Did you talk to John Paul?" Ember asked.

"No, I didn't. According to Elder and Mrs. Smythe, he's a few yards short of a touchdown. Well, those are my words, not theirs."

"In other words," Ember said, "he's mentally challenged. Is that what you're saying, Mr. Sovern?"

"Uh, yeah, sure. Anyway, I convinced Jager to just put the case to bed."

"What if Mary Lou makes a fuss?" Neal asked.

Sovern shrugged. "Jager and I will tell her we're working on it."

"I hope that pacifies her," Harry said.

"The wheel of justice turns but does so slowly."

Neal laughed. "Until someone important enough says otherwise."

Sovern nodded. "But then things do disappear."

Neal shook his head, then asked, "So what do you think happened, Sovern?"

"This is all just a guess. No one is talking who is still around to talk. However, I think Effie Snyder is the one who killed the Middlebrook woman. I'm also thinking she may have done so with her son's help. Maybe used that old pickup truck that Elder Smythe owns. I suppose I could have forensics go over it, but why? Effie's dead and the son probably wouldn't be prosecuted anyway, and, even if he was, I doubt he'd be convicted and why put the Smythe's and the son through all that?"

"Who do you think had it in for Mary Lou?" Harry asked.

"Again, my money's on Effie," Sovern said. "I'm thinking you were right, Thurgood. She killed Louisa Middlebrook to not only send a message to Mary Lou Fight, but to also get revenge for the Middlebrook woman's treatment of her. She hurts Mary Lou, but also sees it as a bit of turnabout is fair play. You know, you hurt me, I hurt you."

"Don't forget," Ember said, "in Effie's mind she was the servant of the Lord, protecting His Anointed."

Sovern nodded. "Yeah, there's that, too. But Effie Snyder isn't the whole story. I think the Walter woman got Terrell Williams to run you down, Thurgood. To get rid of competition concerning the Reverend here. Only he nearly botched the thing. Bet she gave him hell for that. If he'd have hit you both, that would've flushed all her plans down the toilet."

"Makes sense," Neal said. "Makes real good sense."

"Is there any proof of Jessamine's, ah, proclivities?" Harry asked.

"You mean other than the Hayden woman's say so?" Sovern asked.

Harry nodded.

Neal shook his head, and Sovern said, "No."

"So we're really just dealing with a hypothesis here," Harry said.

"That's it, Thurgood," Sovern concurred.

"Well, maybe now things will get back to normal," Harry said.

"Hopefully," Sovern said. "Tourist season is coming up. Don't need extra problems. Well, folks, best get back to my desk." He finished his coffee and left.

"I better get going, too," Neal said. "Got a paper to get out. Let's hope Reece is right: our once in a decade excitement is over and we can get back to business as usual. Well, until May, that is. Although, circulation was up. And I do like that. Talk to you later."

Harry and Ember watched him leave.

"Very sad how all this ended," she said.

"That is true. Very true. But perhaps that swift conclusion was best. Trials take forever, and the humiliation for the people involved would be beyond bearing."

"I just hope both of them now have peace."

"Let's hope so."

They finished their coffee, sat for a moment in silence, and then Ember said she had best get going.

"May I take you out to dinner tonight?"

"Harry, I really don't I think that's a good idea. People talk and I can't afford giving Mary Lou any more ammunition."

"Then how about this: marry me. That will end all the talk."

"What?"

"Marry me, Em. I love you, and I want you to be my wife."

Epilogue

MARY LOU AND GUNTER Fight left the Methodist Church and started attending the Presbyterian Church. The official reason was that the Presbyterian Church was more wheelchair friendly, and seeing that Mary Lou was confined to a wheelchair, and would be for quite some time, "It only makes sense," Gunter had said.

After her second surgery, the doctors were optimistic that with extended physical therapy, there was a good chance she'd be able to walk again in a year and be mostly back to normal in two.

As for the Crimson Hat Society, when Scarlett Hayden quit, and Betty Sue Fernhope returned to the Church of Christ, Mary Lou quietly disbanded the group. But not quietly enough. For in the next edition of the *Chronicle*, the headline screamed, "Crimson Hat Society Dissolved!" And that made Mary Lou very angry.

The Crimson Hat Society of Magnolia Bluff, Texas is alive and well. Mary Lou has seen to that. And it is, of course, very much under her control.

Ember told Harry that she could not marry him. Her words were, "The past is not dead and gone, Harry. It's not even past. Faulkner was right. And I live everyday with my past. I love you, but I can't marry you."

When Harry protested, she didn't argue. She simply said, "We're friends. Best friends." And walked out of the coffee shop.

Later, when she was lying in bed, she cuddled Wilbur, and cried herself to sleep. And did so for many weeks after his proposal.

Two weeks after Harry made his proposal to Ember, he paid Scarlett a visit. He fully expected her to slap his face. Instead, she kissed him. And the kiss wasn't very chaste.

Of course she didn't hate him, she said, and to show him she didn't, she made pizza for him. And she was right: she made a darn good pizza.

The two of them listened to music, made small talk, and danced. But he refused her invitation to stay the night.

"Ember," she said, and Harry nodded.

When he got home and after he'd climbed into bed, he thought of the Reverend Ember Cole. She was his best friend, as well as the woman he loved. He looked towards his window, and whispered, "Dream a little dream of me."

Afterword

I hope you enjoyed *Death Wears a Crimson Hat*. If you did, please leave a review where you bought the book and on your favorite social media sites. Your review is like word of mouth advertising. And it is pure gold.

Become one of my VIP Readers. You'll get a free copy of *Vampire House and Other Early Cases of Justinia Wright, P.I.* and a monthly newsletter announcing other goodies from my pen, as well as curated good reads. And be the first to know about the next release in the Magnolia Bluff Crime Chronicles!

Sign up today for your free book at BookFunnel! Just scan the QR code!

Eulogy in Black and White

The Magnolia Bluff Crime Chronicles continues with *Eulogy in Black and White* by Caleb Pirtle III, which is coming to a bookseller near you soon. Enjoy an excerpt right now!

Eulogy in Black and White
Book 2: The Magnolia Bluff Crime Chronicles

Wednesday
9:22 a.m.

THE NEWSROOM Of the *Magnolia Bluff Chronicle* smells like ink and paper. This morning's ink. Last week's paper. Some swear all news smells, and I won't argue with them. Everybody wants the truth. Very few are willing to tell it. And those who do are generally run out of town. Let's all live a lie, and none of us will get stung. Let a poor boy go to jail, and it's front-page news. Let an advertiser have a closed-door meeting with the judge, and the report winds up in the trash, burned and the ashes scattered somewhere in the next county. A man may bury his conscience, but it will always come back to haunt him. I know. I live with the ghosts.

Nobody, with the exception of Rebecca Wilson, bothers to look up when I walk through the door. She's tall. She's brunette. She could have walked in from the cover of some magazine. Rebecca was probably a cheerleader and quite possibly the Homecoming Queen a few years back. She was definitely a heartbreaker but stayed around while most of her classmates left town for college or better paying jobs until she looked up one morning and there were no hearts left in Magnolia Bluff to break. I'd be willing to let her break mine, but I'm not sure my heart made the trip back from Iraq when I did. I'd at least appreciate Rebecca looking for it, but what would either one of us do if she found it? She wouldn't want it, and I'd just throw it away again.

Rebecca is the receptionist, the society editor, and the head of advertising sales. You want your daughter's wedding picture on the front page? Buy an ad. Want a photograph of your grandchild's graduation tucked prominently in the newspaper and above the fold, buy an ad. Want Rebecca to throw away the cell phone shots of you dancing naked at a biker's bar in Austin, buy an ad. Rebecca Wilson is a top-of-the-line sales lady. She makes more money than the publisher and deserves every cent she can stuff into the bank. She knows who's having a shotgun wedding, who's getting divorced, who's involved in which extracurricular activity at the high school, which preacher has given up booze for smack, who's pregnant, and who the real father is.

Rebecca winks, and her smile can light up a dismal room. She's not flirting. It's her way of saying hello without breaking the cold, deadly, morning silence of a newspaper office that has all personality of a funeral parlor.

"Lose your umbrella?" she asks quietly.

"Didn't think it was supposed to rain."

Her laughter sounds like the black keys on a piano. "Where'd you get that idea?"

"Read in the newspaper somewhere."

Neal Holland grunts loudly. He's the owner, publisher, editor, and guiding genius behind the *Chronicle*. He's bent over the twenty-four-inch screen of his ink-stained IMac Pro, either writing the news or making it up as he goes. I'm told he's good at both.

"Sounds like insubordination to me," he says without looking toward me.

"That's what my Colonel said."

"He shoot you?"

"He tried."

"Close range?"

"From one side of the room to the other."

"That's the reason," Neal says.

"Reason for what?"

"Reason we can't win a damn war." He stops typing long enough to straighten the ragged end of his white mustache. "Damn brass can't shoot straight."

Neal Holland is as close to being a legend as anyone who has ever walked the town square of Magnolia Bluff. He must be in his sixties, but maybe he's older, and his very presence can strike fear into the self-appointed power brokers of Burnet County. Mister Holland is a little too short, a little too round, and his face looks like a rock boulder after sparring with a stick of dynamite. His white hair is always in need of a haircut. His white mustache is a little too shaggy. His eyesight is failing. His dark-rimmed glasses are coke bottle thick. And nobody wants to get on the bad side of a small-town editor who loves nothing better than a good fight.

He's dug up dirt on politicians who have wallowed in a lot of dirt, had the chief of police arrested, the district attorney disbarred, and I know at least three members of the city council who always find out before the meeting which way Neal Holland wants them to vote. They may get out-voted from time to time, but none of them is ever crucified in front-page headlines or skinned alive in print. They have learned the golden rule of small-town journalism. Don't ever pick a fight with a man who buys ink by the barrel and will use as much as he needs to soundly whip you as often as he needs on page one.

I'm standing there with floodwaters dripping off my denim jacket. My jeans are soaked. And the toes of my boots are smeared with mud and charcoal. My hair is plastered dark like shoe polish against my head. A puddle is forming around my feet. And nobody cares. I was hired to sweep the floor, mop it when it's wet, push a button on the old Web-Offset Press every Thursday afternoon and Saturday morning to print six thousand, four hundred, and twenty-two newspapers, then clean the presses before I go home each day. Doesn't pay much. But I only work as hard as I want, and Mister Holland pays me enough to eat twice a day at the Silver Spoon café and rent a place to stay in Nell Walker's three-room boarding house over behind the football field. On most nights, it's quiet. In May, it's so quiet you can hear the mosquitoes mating. But on Friday nights in the autumn, when football is as holy and sanctified as a ladies' prayer meeting at the First Baptist Church, it sounds like an Assembly of God Revival meeting: music, madness, and mayhem.

"You know where the mop is," Mister Holland tells me.

"Pressroom closet."

"Might as well put it to work."

The rain grows louder as it peppers against the building's tin roof. Sounds like a snare drum. I know. I live behind the football field.

The newsroom is about as spare as a room can get. Big plate glass window across the front, looking out on the front lawn of the old rock courthouse, has the name of the newspaper printed in bold white letters with a tagline that says: "The Truth, The Whole Truth, And All The Truth That's Fit To Print, So Help Me God," which is a glorified way of saying: "In this newspaper, you'll find all the news that Neal Holland and his ad-selling assassin believe is fit to print."

The office is no larger than a good-sized bedroom, just big enough for Mister Holland and Rebecca to have a desk with a third desk shoved into the back corner. It's only used by Thomas Hedrick, the owner of the Firestone Tire Store, who writes the game stories about the Magnolia Bluff Bulldog football games. They have not lost a game for the last five years, although time has run out on them twenty-two times.

Hedrick is given forty-two column inches for each game, not counting the statistics, of which there are legion. The Kennedy Assassination had a total of twenty-six column inches, and the 9/11 attack on the Twin Towers scratched out thirty-four column inches. Magnolia Bluff's heart lies in football, not politics, and any story that takes place as far away as twelve miles outside the city limits is considered political and probably a conspiracy theory, not worthy of Neal Holland's trouble.

As I run the mop beside his desk, I can tell the day did not start well, nor will it be ending well. Mister Holland has broken two yellow pencils with his hands and is chewing on a third as if it were a toothpick. His face is red, his eyes narrowed to a stare a sharp as the pointed end of a scalpel. He leans back in his chair, and his gaze moves across the ceiling from one spider web to the next. I offered to sweep the webs away the first week I was on the job, but Mister Holland said no. He likes the spiders. They may be, he says, the only ones in town who truly understand him. Perhaps he's right. He sleeps in the newsroom as often as they do.

Rebecca shoots a frayed rubber band that slaps Mister Holland upside the face. His head jerks around. He's scowling.

"What's wrong, boss," she says.

He waits to see if she is laughing at him.

She isn't.

A deep concern has worked its way into the crystal blue of her eyes.

"Trying to decide the lead article for Thursday's paper," he says, sitting up straight, his elbows on his desk. "We've got the running horse auction out at the barn, and Luis Salas swears he bought himself a Kentucky Derby winner for less than twenty-five thousand dollars. And the city council voted to build a new marina out at the reservoir but looks like we may have to raise property taxes to fund it." He pauses and rubs his eyes. "Can't figure out in my mind which story is the most important to our little town."

"If that's all you got," Rebecca says, crossing her legs as the lace hem of a tight red dress slides up her thigh, "then we might as well forget the newspaper and roll out toilet paper Thursday afternoon. "You know Luis won't ever win the Kentucky Derby. I hear he's selling shares to raise enough money to pay for the horse, and he's only twenty-two thousand dollars short as of yesterday about noon. And this is the fourth time in five years the city council has voted to build a new marina, and none of the little twerps has balls big enough to raise property taxes. They're just spinning loose thread in their yo-yo's."

She waits for Mister Holland to respond.

He doesn't.

His shoulders are sagging. The veins are pulsating in his temples.

He picks up a calendar and turns the page. "You know what Monday is," he says.

"I've been dreading it for months." Rebecca turns away. She has the glint of fear etched in her eyes. The blue has turned to mud.

I wait for somebody to say something.

Nobody does.

I wait a couple of minutes more.

It seems longer.

Nothing but silence.
Rebecca and Mister Holland are lost in their own little worlds.
"What's Monday?" I finally ask.
"May Twenty Third."
"God help us," whispers Rebecca.
I barely hear her.
"What happens on May Twenty Third?
Mister Holland turns slowly around.
His face is pale.
His eyes have turned to water.
His hands are trembling.
He drops the calendar on the floor.
"Somebody dies every May Twenty Third," he says.
"Somebody dies somewhere every day,"
"The last one was Judge Amos Fitzsimmons. Drowned in the baptismal tank down at the First Baptist Church," Rebecca says.
"And the one before the judge was caught on the fifty-yard line of the high school football field and shot point blank with a shotgun in the back of the head. Hardly found enough of his skull to bury."
"Here in Magnolia Bluff?"
"Every year for the last eight years." Rebecca has a tear in her voice.
Mister Holland stands and walks slowly to the front door. He watches the rain a moment, then says. "We know there's a funeral coming," he says. "We just don't know who'll be lying in the casket."

About the Magnolia Bluff Crime Chronicles

"A multi-author crime novel series, you say? What is that?"

That's the question I got when I proposed the idea to my fellow Underground Authors.

We'd just collaborated on a short story anthology, and I was interested in taking the idea of collaboration to the next level.

A multi-author series is what happens when a group of authors decides to write a series of novels. In the case of the Magnolia Bluff Crime Chronicles, the Underground Authors decided to create a fictional town that would be the common denominator for each of the books in the series.

Each author would have his or her characters, perhaps use some of the characters the other authors created, but all of the action would take place in the beautiful little Texas Hill Country town of Magnolia Bluff.

Nine authors showing us nine different sides of the town. We'll experience humor, dark dilemmas, suspense, romance, thrills and spills — all told through a whole lot of good storytelling. The kind that will keep you up past your bedtime, or make you miss your bus stop.

Stay tuned. There's lots happening in Magnolia Bluff. And you don't want to miss any of it.

About the Underground Authors

One afternoon back in June of 2020 I got an email from Caleb Pirtle III inviting me to join an author co-op he was organizing. The purpose of the group would be to promote each other's books. Writing, after all, is easy. Marketing, on the other hand, is difficult. But many hands make light work, and that's what we were hoping for.

In addition to promoting each other's books, and keeping each other up to date on what's happening on the business side of writing, we collaborated on a short story anthology, and are now working on a crime fiction series set in the lovely little Texas Hill Country town of Magnolia Bluff.

The current authors in the underground are Caleb Pirtle III, Linda Pirtle, Cindy Davis, James Callan, Breakfield & Burkey, Kelly Marshall, Richard Schwindt, Jinx Schwartz, Michael Clifton, Ronald E. Yates, Nancy Larson, and CW Hawes.

They are all fine writers and I'm proud to be associated with them.

CW Hawes

About CW Hawes

CW Hawes is a multi-genre author because he is a multi-genre reader. He's penned The Justinia Wright Private Investigator Mysteries, The Rocheport Saga: A Post-Apocalyptic Steam Powered Future, the Pierce Mostyn Paranormal Investigations series, and assorted alternative history and horror offerings.

Born and raised in the Cleveland, Ohio area, CW spent 49 years in the Land of 10,000 Lakes (aka Minnesota), and now proudly hails from the Lone Star State (aka Texas).

He hasn't met a pizza he doesn't like (okay, he detests pineapple), is something of a tea snob, and rocks out to Handel and Vaughan Williams

You can reach him at

Website, just tap, click, or scan the QR code!

Twitter, just tap, click, or scan the QR code!

Facebook, just tap, click, or scan the QR code!

Also by CW Hawes

CW Hawes is a multi-genre author. He currently has work in the mystery, paranormal, horror, post-apocalyptic, and alternative history genres.

You can find all of his work on the My Books page of his website. Just click, tap, or scan the QR code!

Made in the USA
Monee, IL
09 August 2024